Praise for *Anatomy o*
the first book in the Dar.

"If you have any interest in the Victorian era, dark stories, or even just a love of beautiful writing, this is a book you must read."
— Travis West, author of *What Was Left*

"Christie Stratos has taken meticulous care with the use of symbols throughout this story, enhancing her characters with sinister traits that she offsets with unique backstory or extenuating circumstances, blurring the line between good and villain line enough to make this a super compelling read."
— MM Jaye, author of the Greek Tycoons series

"Christie Stratos has written this story in such a wonderful way and brings the 19th century to life…I was completely mesmerized by this slice of the 1800s as Christie presented it to us."
— The Scary Reviews

"The writing is phenomenal. It's not a long book, and the author makes every word count. Her descriptions are perfectly refined to give the reader exactly the amount of detail you need."
— Sunshine Somerville, author of The Kota series

"I loved it. If I had to categorize this work I would say that it is a much darker version of Alcott's work."
— Amazon review

"The author clearly did a lot of research to get her facts right about many different aspects of the Victorian era, right down to details, which gives the story a believable quality and brings it to life. Frighteningly so."
—Autumn (Amazon review)

"There are times when the author delivers moments of sheer sadness of a tragic quality that profoundly moved me. That is not easy to achieve, whatever your talents as a writer...Psychologically compelling and full of depth, intelligent, beautifully written, literary but easily accessible, *Anatomy of a Darkened Heart* may well begin a new era of dark Victorian-era fiction."
—Jason Greensides, author of *The Distant Sound of Violence*

"The psychological twists and turns kept the tension high and the way Christie could get me to sympathize with a character in one chapter and despise them three chapters later was masterfully done."
—Emily S. (Amazon review)

"I liked the natural progression of the story, how each character's darkness stood out more as the story went. It isn't easy to give a character his or her own world while keeping the story in check and allowing for each storyline to merge and form into a coherent piece of masterful awesomeness."
—J.B. Taylor, author of the Dissimilar Shorts series

"This was definitely a book full of intrigue and mystery..."
—Amazon review

ANATOMY OF A DARKENED HEART

CHRISTIE STRATOS

Anatomy of a Darkened Heart: a Dark Victoriana Collection novel (Book 1)
Copyright © Christie Stratos (2015). All Rights Reserved.
First edition.
Published by Proof Positive Publishing
Cover art design: Ebook Launch (http://ebooklaunch.com)
Editing and proofreading services: Proof Positive (http://proofpositivepro.com)

ISBN-13: 978-0-9967812-0-6
ISBN-10: 099678120X

DEDICATION

To my family, who always told me I could do the things I doubted. I could not have come this far without your support, and because of it, I know I can continue. "Thank you" is too pale a phrase.

To my mentor and friend, Dr. Philip Billings, who taught me that fiction is limitless and boundaries simply don't exist. There is, and never will be, anyone like you.

ACKNOWLEDGEMENTS

Doll Doctor Kathleen, your passion and incredible knowledge of dolls throughout the ages was not only invaluable to this book, but it was so interesting. Our chats were inspiring and so much fun.

Elena Greene, your expertise in historical fiction was so helpful for a fact I couldn't find anywhere no matter how hard I looked. Thanks for using your experience to help a new author out.

#Awethors, there aren't enough words to thank you all! I would have been much more afraid of the whole publication process if it hadn't been for all of your support and encouragement. If I ever had a question, I turned to you and got solid answers.

Anita Stratos, my editor from Proof Positive, thank you for all the tiny details you picked out and all the help you gave reworking sections and researching impossibly itsy bitsy facts. I could not have had such an accurate book without you.

Dane from Ebook Launch, you took my (awful) drawing and all my scattered ideas and turned them into a book cover even more perfect than I imagined. Thanks for your attention to detail and eye for darkness.

Part 1

*Thou feedest them with the bread of tears; and givest them
tears to drink in great measure.*

Psalm 80:5
King James Bible

Birth

It was in the very moment of her birth that the ambiance changed. Everyone felt it. The room darkened, blackened to the point that the midwife paused, the baby still half inside her mother, to look around, frowning deeply. Elizabeth's heartbeat quickened.

"The clocks…" the midwife muttered. They had stopped. There were two in the room, and they'd both stopped ticking simultaneously. The midwife looked right into Elizabeth's eyes with an expression that was half apologetic and half frightened. Clocks were only physically stopped—not supernaturally—when someone died or while mourning the deceased. But now the clocks had stopped by themselves, and nobody had died. Unless…

"Is the baby all right?" Elizabeth shrieked, leaning forward as much as possible. She was covered in cold sweat and exhausted and scared.

The midwife suddenly remembered to continue with the birth and gently helped the baby out the rest of the way. It made no sound.

"Is it alive?" Elizabeth was frantic now. This was her first child and if it was stillborn… The midwife wasn't answering. She was just staring at the baby. Elizabeth couldn't even see it. "Is it alive!" she yelled.

"It's alive," the midwife said quietly. She wiped blood off of it slowly as if under some sort of spell. "It's not crying yet, though." She rubbed its belly and it made a sound like recognition, like an annoyed grunt. But it didn't cry. And then the clocks started again with a hard *tick*, but

9

neither woman noticed.

"Is it a girl or a boy?" Elizabeth asked. She was getting irritated now. What was wrong with this midwife?

The midwife looked at her again, that same look on her face, this time with more worry than fear. "A girl," she whispered.

"What's wrong with you? Give her to me!" Elizabeth couldn't take it anymore. This woman wouldn't tell her why she was making that dreadful face and she wasn't giving information freely. They would complain about her. She'd have Richard do it.

"I-I'm sorry. I didn't mean to... It's just that... Well, here." And with that, the midwife stood up, took two long steps around the bed, and harshly held the baby out. Elizabeth took her, not really seeing while she concentrated on taking hold of her properly.

As soon as the little girl was in her arms, against her body, Elizabeth saw it. Tired eyes. Eyes like an adult—an unhappy adult. The blue eyes were like big round teardrops, wide and evaluating, searching for something. Under the bright blue eyes were circles, light gray circles that threatened to darken. Those tired, striking eyes weren't closed or roaming, they were focused on Elizabeth's eyes. It felt as if something was connecting their pupils so that neither of them could look away and neither could blink. Elizabeth felt a sudden strong sadness, loss, disconnect. Something wasn't right with this child. It couldn't be. Children weren't like this. But then again, who's to say they couldn't be? It wasn't squirming either. It just lay there limply and stared into her eyes.

The room never brightened again.

0–6 weeks old
1840

November 1, 1840

Elizabeth had planned to name the child Mary Judith but couldn't bring herself to do it after the clocks stopped, after she'd seen its eyes. They were so strange, those eyes. She couldn't get over how tired the baby looked. It couldn't be normal...

Richard didn't have any interest in the name, so it was up to Elizabeth. Whatever she wanted, he'd said. Anything was fine, he'd said. She knew he wanted a boy. She asked the midwife what his reaction had been when she'd told him it was a girl. The midwife gave her a small, tight smile, a smile that looked like a stretched-out jumprope in the middle of play, and then looked down. He wasn't pleased.

Elizabeth knew she had plenty of time to name the baby before it was baptized in four weeks. There was something unsettling about having a living being in the house with no name attached to it. Or perhaps it was just this baby that unsettled her. Perhaps the first should be their last... But she already knew Richard wouldn't accept that. He wanted a boy, and if he wanted it, he would have it.

He hadn't seen her since the birth, hadn't come to visit or even sent a note in with the midwife. Nothing. She felt empty, lonesome, with just this odd, tired, quiet child to keep her company. Actually, there was now a nurse milling about to take care of it while she rested, but she didn't see too much of either nurse or baby. She couldn't even accept visitors for two more weeks. That was a long time to sit in bed, alone. It was a long time.

But back to the name. What should she call it? Elizabeth breathed deeply and pulled the covers up further. She was half sitting, half lying slouched in bed, pillows messily spread out behind her. She liked the covers all the way up to her shoulders. It was October and chillier than usual. A weak fire crackled in the fireplace across from her bed. She wanted tea, boiling hot tea to hold in her hands, against her chest so she could feel the steam rise up to her chin.

Abigail.

The name came to her suddenly, just popped into her mind like it was meant to be. *Abigail.*

Did she know anyone named Abigail? Or was it a name she recalled from her Bible readings? Well...honestly...she didn't read it often, if at all anymore. Her memory was terrible, so whenever anyone quoted from the Bible, she smiled and nodded piously, as if she knew exactly where the quote came from, as if she could remember all those pages word by word. She was supposed to know them. She didn't.

Abigail was a good woman, she thought. A wife, twice. Perhaps if the first name represented someone decent, a woman with morals, the child would follow suit.

But Richard's distance from this child made Elizabeth want to do something to make him sorry he wasn't taking an interest. It would satisfy a loving, warm side of her that was always being pushed down by him. A little secret her daughter may never understand, but Richard certainly would. It could be something Elizabeth could call her when she was frustrated with Richard. Perhaps she could force him to care that way, so she could say, "You should have taken more of an interest in our daughter when she was first born. If you'd only done that..." and she could finish that sentence whatever way suited the situation.

Delilah.

Delilah was a lovely name, a name that carried betrayal of a man. It was perfect. It was Elizabeth's permanent private revenge.

November 1, 1840—one day after birth
Richard Whitestone's diary

Abigail Delilah Whitestone.

That is to be the baby's name.

Delilah.

I don't know where Elizabeth gets her cruel streak. Her mother was impeccably moral and stern, the way a mother and wife should be. And yet, she has decided on this name. This clearly ominous name. This will surely set our daughter up to be something despicable.

I told Elizabeth I wanted a boy, not a girl. I was explicit. And yet she did not pray hard enough. Perhaps she should not have stayed home from church for her sickness in the morning. Perhaps the Lord is angry with me for allowing it, and He has now punished me with a girl. I don't want to see it. I wouldn't know what to do with it. Who will inherit our estate now? Someone from outside the family. Elizabeth will have to continue her wifely duties to me until she gives me a boy. She owes me that.

Who will trust a woman with the middle name of Delilah? Certainly no one in our church-going town. I will speak to Elizabeth soon, although I am still too disgusted to see her. Her lack of piousness shows in the sex of our baby —and its unfortunate name.

She will bend. She will have to.

November 9, 1840

Elizabeth waited for days, but Richard didn't come to see her. The nurse kept her in bed to ensure her health. The maid, Ashdon, brought her everything she needed. She had nothing to complain about. Except Richard.

"Has he seen the baby yet?" Elizabeth asked every single day for two weeks. Every single day the nurse shook her head, breaking eye contact, answering the ground.

All she had received so far was a note from Richard two days after the birth. It read:

Elizabeth,

"Delilah" is wrong. I am sure you will make a decision more apt for moral fortitude. I am sure you will realize your mistake. Prove yourself to me and rename it.

Richard

Realize her mistake? Prove herself? What horrible things to say to a new mother.

She *would* prove herself.

"Good afternoon, Mrs. Hinsley. It's wonderful to see you," Elizabeth said as Mrs. Victoria Hinsley entered the visiting room. Elizabeth held the baby on her lap, bouncing it lightly. The nurse had put it in a clean white robe, which was both agreeable and disturbing because it brought out the baby's under-eye circles. Pale skin, pale eyes, dark circles.

"Good afternoon, Mrs. Whitestone. I'm so happy to see your little one!" Mrs. Hinsley came closer, smiling brightly, all clenched teeth. Mrs. Hinsley was barren. Pretty Mrs. Hinsley, whom all the young men had clamored after.

"Yes, I'm very glad to be receiving again."

Mrs. Hinsely paused when she was just a few feet away. She'd noticed the baby's eyes too. It was unnatural. Her smile faltered.

"She's just lovely," she said, voice wavering accidentally on the last word. She tried to keep her poise but backed up a step. It was a natural reaction. "Oh," she said, turning around, "I thought the chair was closer." She didn't think the chair was closer. Not really. Strolling over to the chair across from Elizabeth, Mrs. Hinsley sat down, keeping her eyes on her knees. "How are you feeling, dear?"

"Oh, very well," Elizabeth said. It was true that her health was good. Her heart… "It does something to you, having a baby. I feel more refreshed than with a thousand nights of sleep." Not true either.

"And have you and Mr. Whitestone chosen a name for the child yet? I know the baptism isn't for another two weeks, but—"

"Abigail."

"What a beautiful name! Not so extraordinarily popular, but certainly pretty. She'll stand out for sure." Mrs. Hinsley lifted her head in a self-righteous manner.

"Abigail Delilah."

A pause.

"Oh." Mrs. Hinsley frowned ever so slightly, her pretty face looking both worried and pleased, like she wasn't completely positive whether she'd won a game of chess. "How…how delightful." Her grin assured Elizabeth the name would spread around town very quickly.

"Just like her," Elizabeth said.

She didn't truly know yet the irony of her statement.

*

Elizabeth received more visitors than expected during the two weeks before the baptism. She was the only woman in town who had named her baby an oxymoron. Everyone was fascinated.

During every visit, the questions started out very general: "How did you pick the names?" "Did Mr. Whitestone help?" "Is either name after your mother?" Then they become more pointed: "Why those particular names? Neither is really popular." "How did you ever decide on those two names? Aren't they quite opposites?" "My dear, what possessed you? Sweet to the ear, yes, but what will everyone think of their meaning?"

Richard was miserable. He'd had to start talking to her once visitations were to begin. The very night before at nine o'clock, he'd knocked gently on her door. When she didn't answer regardless of the glow of light that showed plainly beneath the door, he pounded heavily, angrily. He entered without waiting for her invitation.

"Visitations begin tomorrow, Elizabeth," he said, already sounding irritated as if they were continuing an argument they'd had in person just minutes before. "What have you decided regarding the child's name?" He stood at the door, closing it only partially. He didn't bother to go over to her. He didn't bother to ask how she was, show her some warmth. He stood as if an affront had already occurred, his shoulders squared, his legs spread in a sturdy stance. Even his mustache looked stiff and aggressive. She wished she had continued working as bookkeeper at the *Advocate for Moral Reform* and taken care of her parents instead of marrying.

"Don't worry, dear. I'll prove myself," was all she said before looking down at the book she had been reading. He remained, unmoving, for five long moments, just staring harshly. She could see his hazel eyes, their intense determination boring into her, without even looking up. She refused to look up. If she did, she might shrivel from his coldness.

He finally left.

There had been a time when Elizabeth mistook Richard's coldness for rigid logic and extreme piety. She hadn't seen any affection from him before they got married, but that wasn't unusual in their circles. He never tried to steal a kiss or hold her on the rare occasion that others were out of the room for even just a moment, but she'd thought that meant he had a great deal of respect for her. And when they were together at night there was never, not even on their honeymoon abroad, an actual interest in *her*, regardless of the proof of their child. He did not express love in any way. She realized now that none of it had been normal. She had yearned for it, brushed his hand with hers

18

before marriage and pulled him into kisses after, but in both he pulled away. He only cared for what the Bible said a man and woman should mean to each other: children. He didn't seem to know what a home was, what it represented. Just his interpretation of his treasured religious book, the words he heard in church. Or at least that was all she could see. He was a rock, and she realized now he would never be different, not even with the birth of their first child.

She continued to read his Bible, the precious book he'd abandoned just to sleep in another room for days. She read Judges carefully and underlined just as cautiously, making sure not to accidentally run her lines into a single word. And unconsciously, her mouth slowly curled into something resembling a smile.

December 13, 1840
Richard Whitestone's diary

Elizabeth has told everyone she knows that the baby's middle name is Delilah. I cannot express my disappointment in her. She is not the pure woman her mother was.

I had the new wallpaper put up in time for the baptism. It is the most wonderful flocked wallpaper, black damask on a stunning pure white. I've had it put up along the staircase and in the second floor hallway. It represents her. It represents what she has created in this child. It matches the wide half-moons beneath the child's eyes.

I did not bother to ask what she thought as her opinion is irrelevant. I already know she will hate it as she dislikes anything too dark. Even wearing mourning clothes is something unsavory to her. When her mother died, she wore the darkest shade of purple far too soon. It should have been black and nothing but black for much longer. But she cannot stand such darkness. Ironic.

I have come to a conclusion. If her spirit is truly lowered by the wallpaper's heaviness, she will need to seek spiritual counsel at our place of worship—that is the only logical thing to do. She must do that anyway, and this would push her without my having to do so outwardly. If she sees the wallpaper's representation of her, of the bright purity in every woman but which she is hiding under a bushel of darkness, she will not say anything. In that case, she may need to be committed so that the child may be cared for by a more suitable mother.

We shall see if she is repentant.

In the meantime, we must christen this child together in

our house.

I have chosen appropriate godparents for Abigail. (Here in my own diaries, that shall be her only name.) Mr. and Mrs. Hinsley will be perfect, especially since they could advance her social standing, and they have no child of their own. God has not deemed Mrs. Hinsley suitable for her own children, and while that is unfortunate, it means Abigail will have godparents with more means than they would have had otherwise. Since Mrs. Hinsley is barren, perhaps she and her husband will be gracious enough to promise some of their fortune to Abigail in their wills. She will need all the help she can get, being set up in this world with such a poor name. It will surely affect her.

I am getting far ahead of myself.

The Hinsleys will make perfect godparents.

*

The Hinsleys. Godparents.

Elizabeth knew what he was thinking. He was thinking they would grant Abigail Delilah plenty of gifts, money, bestow upon her all the things they could not give their own baby. But he was also thinking Mrs. Hinsley could act as a second mother to the child, replace Elizabeth even if only to a small degree. He was thinking Mrs. Hinsley would make Elizabeth into the woman he wanted her to be: her mother.

She would be no such thing.

Elizabeth's mother was a pious woman, yes, but also hard, cold, so stern that Elizabeth never felt her love. Exactly what she married into. *How do these horrible motifs carry through a person's life?* If she had already experienced distance from her parents, should she not experience warmth from her husband? Was that not what was due her?

It seemed not.

Elizabeth wondered… If she was more like Mrs. Hinsley, would Richard change at all? Would he become more considerate, more caring? Elizabeth doubted it. More likely he would remain the same but approve of her more. *What does that feel like?* She supposed it must feel like a child winning a game of fox and geese—hard won and short-lived. Insignificant in the long run.

No, she would not be her mother's daughter.

She must take Mrs. Hinsley in, make her think that she was welcome in Elizabeth's home at all times, that she was part of the Whitestone family now. Now that Richard had already made this enormous decision and informed them behind Elizabeth's back, she must make Mrs. Hinsley feel like she belonged, bring her in close. That would be the easiest way to eliminate her from the picture.

Richard had changed the wallpaper. It was horrid. Black damask on blinding white. She would have preferred almost anything else. But why would he ask her? It was his house.

It *was* his house.

It was *his* house.

It was *his* baby.

But it was in *her* hands.

*

Mrs. Hinsley walked around the jeweler's shop looking for the perfect gift for her new goddaughter, Abigail... Delilah...Whitestone. She'd told her husband not to bother coming since it would be such a bore to him. As usual he hadn't fussed about it. In fact he hadn't even answered. Just turned the page of his newspaper. It was probably a relief for him.

The jeweler's shop was small but had a large selection. This was where Mr. Hinsley bought Victoria's birthday presents and anniversary presents. Almost always something made of pearls. In fact she wore a gold-set cameo, a carving of herself that her husband had commissioned, carved out of pure white shell untinged with the brown that can sometimes mar a perfect cameo. The gold frame was studded with pearls and diamonds, the perfect first anniversary present. He had put it at her place for her to find at dinner, and when she'd discovered it, she'd felt a sinking feeling that was quite unexpected. The smile that she felt stretch her skin had been plastered on out of courtesy. She'd found out just a couple of weeks earlier that she couldn't have children. She was a useless woman, only worth anything for her literal wealth, nothing more. She could never perform her wifely duties to ultimate satisfaction.

Victoria had told her husband that the cameo brooch was the most beautiful thing she had ever seen—and it was. It was the kindest gift she'd ever received. And who knew an artist could be so talented as to carve a cameo based on a likeness? She'd always thought the model had to be there in person. Daguerrotypes could be so vague, sometimes eliminating the bridge of one's nose or the severity of their cheekbones. But this artist had made a brilliant likeness of her.

She remembered crying despite herself in that moment. The servants had withdrawn at a wave of her husband's hand to spare her the embarrassment. She had explained, across the long dining room table while looking down at her plate, that she was barren. A teardrop had landed on her mutton. For some reason, that made her throat clench with even harsher sadness. When she'd heard no response from him, she looked up to find her husband didn't look altogether disappointed.

"That's all right, dear," he'd said. "Another person might get in the way of our routines."

That was all he had said. And the word choice—*person* instead of baby or child?—was completely abnormal. That hadn't escaped her. But Victoria had convinced herself he'd reacted this way because he loved her and didn't want to hurt her with his disappointment, the disappointment he was surely hiding. But he never asked again if she had visited the doctor to see if things had changed. He never asked if there were measures they could take to have a child, or otherwise adopt one. In fact, he'd seemed almost smug the next morning. There was no other word she could put to his demeanor. It was so odd. *Beauty but no baby.* Perhaps that was enough for him. But she knew there was more to it, even then. Now, a year later, she knew better why he hadn't been upset. He knew that no other man would want her.

Victoria wore the brooch of herself at her throat quite often, especially in times of mild self-doubt. She had an idea of what she wanted to get the Whitestone child, but she hadn't decided until she'd gotten to the jewelry shop and seen the perfect thing.

The gift was a bit unusual, in fact quite out of the ordinary, but appropriate in her own opinion. Expensive enough that Mrs. Whitestone couldn't possibly reject it at the baptism in front of everyone. It would cause that in-between feeling brought on by public realization, the feeling between hatred and helplessness. A grasping feeling with no end and no solution. And she would be stuck with it forever.

A painted eye motif on ivory set in ornate gold. A brooch the child could wear at her neck, over her heart, throughout her life. A symbol of Mr. Whitestone's infidelity. A constant reminder to Mrs. Whitestone of her inadequacy as a woman, regardless of her ability to bear children.

Mrs. Whitestone may have the child, but she didn't have the man.

She never would.

*

How could Mrs. Hinsley's husband let her give something like that to a baby, especially in front of all those people? How could *either* husband let it happen?

Elizabeth was humiliated, outraged. That barely controlled sort of outrage that showed on her face through a mask of wide, black-hole eyes, eyes that could chew up their victim, mouth in a stiff sort of smile like a bracket on its side, like half a square—the bottom half.

Elizabeth's fingers had gripped the brooch tightly, pinching it between her forefinger and thumb, the small bit of skin it touched completely white from the pressure.

When she put it down on the table hard enough to scratch the surface, blood was left on her finger; the sharp end of the lover's eye pin had stabbed her. She'd had to say thank you. Graciously. Among whispers and stares, following a vicious act, she'd had to show genuine appreciation. She wanted to break it. She wanted to force it into Mrs. Hinsley's Cheshire cat mouth, force her jaw closed, make her choke on it as it scraped its way down her toxic throat and got stuck.

She hadn't known this was going on. But now... The lover's eye in Mrs. Hinsley's eye color was bad enough, but the pearls represented tears—everyone knew that.

A realization pressed at her mind. There was one particular thing that had bothered her for quite some time. Elizabeth had always done the bookkeeping for their family. It was something Richard had once commented on as a particularly "moral" skill of hers, perhaps because it required pure honesty and so few people dealing with money had that quality.

She had done it successfully for two years of their marriage until Richard had asked to see her records. Every once in a while he stood over her while she wrote in her ledger, but he had never actually asked to see them separately before. He had said... What was it... He had said he wanted to analyze their expenses to see if they could hire a better cook, perhaps a butler instead of a maid. Elizabeth had handed him the book with no suspicion, but when it came time to enter a new bill payment, she realized he never returned it.

Several times she had asked to have it back, very simply saying things like, "When you have a chance, just leave the ledger on the table," and later, "I've written down some expenses and payments on the notebook in the desk, so when you return the books, I'll write them in." He would usually hum his acknowledgement, giving no actual answer. Then he got to the point of completely ignoring her.

Finally ten bills and payments had piled up, and when she reminded him yet again and got no response, she had felt a surge of pent-up frustration that came out of her mouth as, "Richard, I am the one who handles our expenses after all. You must give it back. It's very bad practice to keep all these records piling up out of place. I don't even know what the bank balance is anymore."

He'd stood from his chair, put his newspaper down—all quite calmly as ever was—and said, "You have too much pride about the bookkeeping and you've made mistakes. I will do it from now on."

"Well show me where I've made mistakes then. Help me improve," Elizabeth said, aggravation soaking her tone; she knew she hadn't made any mistakes. She'd checked the numbers over and over. This was the one thing she was good at.

"There it is again," Richard said disapprovingly. "Pride. It's a sin, you know."

"Richard, I have no pride. If I have made mistakes, I am asking for the chance to fix them," Elizabeth said, even more irritated by his lack of emotion, lack of care that this mattered to her. He never bothered to see things from her perspective. "You once told me you very much respect my careful handling of our money, and now you are taking that away from me. Do you really expect me to simply agree without a second chance?"

"It is your duty as a wife to obey me," he said. "I say I

will be doing the bookkeeping from now on and you must accept that. I say it is bringing out a sinful side and you must accept that too because I know it to be true. It is not a discussion. I am telling you, and that should be enough."

She'd stood there, feeling like a child scolded by her father, and stared at him with no words to throw back. She was fighting a battle she was not going to win no matter what she said. She could give up on it and have it end there or she could keep pursuing it and make him say even more awful things that weren't true.

In the end she had stomped out of the room feeling impotent and useless. She had run up the stairs and closed the door to their bedroom behind her, locking it from the inside. And then she had taken apart every single drawer, every chest, and every bit of clothing she could find, looking for the ledger. But it was nowhere. She nearly drove herself insane, thinking she must be blind. She was convinced it was in that room, not in the rest of the house, and that it was sleeping beside her every night without her knowledge.

Deciding which drawer to search for the third time, she'd paused and in those few seconds of silence, in those surprisingly long seconds of sweaty exasperation, she recognized the sound of footsteps walking away from the door.

He had been listening. Listening to her tear the room apart inch by inch. He had not knocked nor had he said anything to her. He had just listened.

That was the moment she'd realized she had married something wicked. Everything had changed after that. It had been far from perfect before, but that moment was the end of any trust between them.

Thinking back on all that now, two years later, and remembering it with such vividness, Elizabeth supposed she should not be surprised that their first child was so odd. It was, after all, half his. And now it was starting its life with a brand on it. A pin of betrayal.

No one ever would have known about it if this "gift" hadn't been given, because Mrs. Hinsely was barren and everyone knew it. So there could never be an accident, a questionable child, to prove the horrid sin.

And yet Mrs. Hinsley had done this.

And Richard had stood stolid as ever as Elizabeth had received it, showing no emotion, no fear, no regret. Nothing.

If he thought he would have a son after this, he was badly mistaken. He would have to force her. And that would be a sin.

But then again, so was this.

December 20, 1840

Neither parent would see the baby after Mrs. Hinsley's foul "gift" to Abigail Delilah. The governess was ashamed to work in a household with such a dishonorable man, but she would not leave poor Abigail. She was the only one who looked after her, took care of her—bothered with her at all. She found it so saddening that the parents of any child, no matter what circumstances may surround her, could possibly ignore her so. Abigail would suffer in her upbringing, surely. The governess's own care, even though she had accepted a continuing role as governess from Mr. Whitestone, was simply not enough, not equal to the attention of a natural parent. It was their responsibility to God and to the child to raise her properly, show her some amount of love and compassion. It was their responsibility to determine her future, not only in fortune but in character.

They would all realize their sins in their return to their Maker.

Perhaps sooner.

6 weeks–2 years old
1841–1842

January 20, 1841

Elizabeth stood on the stairs, facing the wall, only a foot away. Her finger roamed over a section of the black pattern, feeling the difference between the black and the white. There was a tangible distinction—they were not the same. Not the same at all. Her finger moved across the change in color over and over and over…

"Elizabeth," Richard said loudly, forcefully. She always felt disobedient when he spoke. He was wearing his incredulous frown, the one that insinuated she was stupid. The one he seemed to always wear these days. He used to wear a why-do-you-insist-on-affection frown most of the time, one-third sorry, one-third annoyed, one-third pitying.

She was good at measuring expressions, especially his.

She dropped her hand from the wallpaper and turned to face Richard.

"What were you doing?" he demanded.

"What are the two materials used to make the wallpaper?" she asked. She had something in mind.

He stared blankly at her. No, not blankly. Not blankly at all. Distinctly panicked deep inside, behind his mask.

"What was that?" He wasn't comprehending, or rather, he was probably hoping his comprehension was incorrect. It wasn't.

"The materials that make up the wallpaper. There's one material for the black pattern and one for the white background. I'd like to know what they are. I'd like to have a dress made from fabrics to imitate them. Something similar to this beautiful pattern." She held a grin back behind her teeth, the inner cavern of her mouth yawning at him, her lips steady and straight as if nothing was happening inside.

He continued to stare.

"I think I'll get white satin with black velvet," she said and started to turn up the stairs but kept her eyes on his.

He was afraid. She could see it clearly now.

"Perhaps Mrs. Hinsley should have one as well," she said, then floated up.

She is exactly what I feared. Unrepentant. But not just that, it is beyond that. She seems to revel in the wickedness in herself that the wallpaper represents. She wants to wear a dress with the same pattern and colors, a replica for her body. I feel more than disappointment now. I am shocked to feel fear. There is a devil in that woman and I do not know how to eradicate it.

I wrote to a home for disturbed women today, asking for the requirements to commit someone. I have no evidence to submit her, but surely there must be another way. They must be aware that not everyone leaves proof of their wrongdoings. But then again, she works through veiled threats. I do not even have the proof of fainting spells.

I am less worried for little Abigail than I am for myself. At least Abigail has a nursemaid to keep Elizabeth at bay. I do not have that luxury.

*

Elizabeth knew that Mrs. Hinsley would call on her soon. Every day she waited in the parlor in a beautiful day dress that was quite the latest, sometimes with lightly patterned layers in the skirt, sometimes with a plunging neckline filled with a delicate chemisette. Elizabeth owned the dresses, but they were for Mrs. Hinsley's benefit. Elizabeth would never have worn quite such fashionable things, and perhaps Richard would have respected her more for it, but she was through with trying to please him. She would now take control and become the one not to be trifled with.

The Whitestone servants were ready every afternoon to bring out Indian tea in the beautiful sterling silver set with the swing kettle that had been Elizabeth's wedding present from her mother. Her mother had probably figured Elizabeth's worth would come from Richard's ability to sell it if he wasn't pleased with Elizabeth herself. That was what her mother had thought of her on their wedding day: as lacking and in need of something material to improve her worth.

Elizabeth had ordered the servants to have cream instead of milk ready for Mrs. Hinsley—this was the trend now. And small sugar cubes. Everything was constantly at the ready, waiting for Mrs. Hinsley. Waiting and waiting. Others visited, and for them the servants knew to bring the regular tea set. Richard wouldn't have approved at all of her using the silver unless it was for someone important—he didn't like to put on airs and he didn't like for anyone to think of him as anything but pious. The silver tea set was "a curse of a gift", Richard had said, and he couldn't understand why her mother had given it to them. She thought he would sell it since he found no need for it, but he didn't seem to care enough to bother. Yet.

Richard had always been hypocrisy after hypocrisy, marrying an affectionate woman when he wanted a cold thing. And then turning his affections to another. He was truly impossible.

But this meeting would change things. This meeting would put Elizabeth back where she belonged in Mrs. Hinsley's esteem. It would point out Mrs. Hinsley's lack of dignity without saying anything outright. And that was always the best way.

Mrs. Hinsley finally visited Elizabeth on a Monday—January 24, to be exact. When Ashdon came into the sitting room to announce Mrs. Hinsley's arrival, Elizabeth took great joy in not getting up to greet her. Mrs. Hinsley did stumble over that, and she paused awkwardly before walking over to the couch and sitting down.

"How are you, dear?" Mrs. Hinsley asked, arranging her skirts unnecessarily.

"Oh very well," Elizabeth gushed. "My little Abigail is such a joy. She's already given Richard and me so much pleasure."

"Oh?" Mrs. Hinsley asked, looking around the room.

"You know, I never realized how empty Christmas was without a baby." Elizabeth hoped her words were needles in Mrs. Hinsley's delicate skin. "Everything is so much more lively and worship is so much deeper with a new life in the house."

"Mmm, how nice."

"I'm sure *Mr.* Hinsley will want to spend plenty of time with Abigail since…well, you know." Elizabeth scrunched her nose and nodded as if they were good friends avoiding an inappropriate subject about a mutual acquaintance. She was being far more direct than she'd planned. She'd wanted to seem dignified and arrogant, to make Mrs. Hinsley worried that the baby was bringing Richard and Elizabeth closer, that Mrs. Hinsley was no longer wanted by Richard. But these direct attacks were indelicate. It was as if her inner core of hatred for Mrs. Hinsley was expelling itself through her pointed words, but it wasn't giving Elizabeth the relief she'd assumed it would. No, instead the core was growing with each line she spewed that didn't seem to affect Mrs. Hinsley. Of course Elizabeth noticed the lack of eye contact from Mrs. Hinsley, but she had hoped to see some more obvious pain. Instead she was left feeling as if she were a scone that had been dipped in salt rather than sugar while Mrs. Hinsley was a fragile, sweet wafer. It made her red core of hatred expand.

"Your nursemaid must be quite adequate," Mrs. Hinsley said. "Richard told me he hired one recommended by the church."

A double slap to the face. First calling Elizabeth's husband by his first name, then… Richard hadn't told Elizabeth where he'd gotten the recommendation for the nursemaid or even that he'd gotten a recommendation in the first place.

"Yes, she's quite adequate," Elizabeth said, hearing her voice stiffening. She had to say it now, before she exploded. "My dear, I've gotten you a present." She could only use such a sweet term of endearment because she knew what was coming.

"Oh? Really, you shouldn't have. If anything I should be buying you more things for little Abigail."

The term "little Abigail" sickened Elizabeth. It made her hate the carefully chosen name. Elizabeth stood.

"Now just wait there a moment while I get it," she said, and left the room.

There were two kinds of thumping going on in Elizabeth's heart as she walked to retrieve the gift. One thump was excitement over finally having something clever with which to trump this woman. It was a thump similar to the kind when a brilliant Christmas present was finally being opened by its recipient. The other thump was anxiety over whether this would help the situation or make it much worse. This gift could either ensure Mrs. Hinsley stayed at a distance for the embarrassment it should cause her, or she would pursue her affair further, if she was stubborn enough. At this point, Elizabeth just wanted to trump her.

She slid the large gift off the table and onto her hands, the cold, flat surface of its bottom feeling especially solid now that the time had come. She paused and looked at the wrapping covering the whole thing but stopping just shy of the bottom. *Wolf in sheep's clothing...*

But this woman deserved it. And could it really be a sin to potentially hurt her when Elizabeth was really just trying to put a stop to this woman's sin? For God's sake, Mrs. Hinsley was breaking one of the ten commandments. Wasn't it Elizabeth's right to stop her, not just because it hurt Elizabeth, but because obviously neither Mrs. Hinsley nor Richard could stop themselves from committing such sin? How could it be wrong?

Elizabeth took one step, then another, and another until she had finally taken enough steps to get to the sitting room where Mrs. Hinsley waited. She didn't know why her conscience was fighting her, but she did everything possible to push it down so she could enjoy this moment.

She placed the gift on the table between herself and Mrs. Hinsley.

"I hope you like it," Elizabeth said, smiling. She felt the anticipation of giving a brilliant present again.

"I can't imagine!" Mrs. Hinsley said, seeming excited. She slid to the edge of the couch and put her hands on the gathered brown paper at the top of the gift. Elizabeth's heart almost hurt with its sudden jolt of nerves, and now it pounded loudly. Finally Mrs. Hinsley lifted the paper up and off the present—and stared, a flicker of confusion on her face.

"A birdcage?" she asked quietly. Elizabeth couldn't tell if she truly didn't grasp it or if she already understood it inside and out and was in shock.

"Yes," Elizabeth said breathlessly. "I thought perhaps since you can't have... Instead you could have a little birdie or two for company." Elizabeth could feel her smile hurting from its excessive width. "And you could pick the most beautiful one, so that you're completely equal."

There it was. On Mrs. Hinsley's face. Recognition. And anger. Her pretty little features were finally distorted.

Elizabeth felt as if she had waited years for this moment. After she'd left more than enough time for Mrs. Hinsley to thank her, which she didn't, Elizabeth finished with, "It will be nice to have so much in common."

*

Victoria didn't know how to explain the birdcage to her husband when she returned home directly after opening the present. Even the Hinsleys' butler, Collins, looked at it oddly.

"Shall I take that for you, madam?" he asked, betraying his confusion only through his barely pursed lips. He was flawless in his job, and Victoria didn't know whether she had a right to feel angry over his minor, almost imperceptible reaction. She didn't answer him right away, fighting what she realized more by the millisecond was unjustified rage toward him. Instead she put on a tight smile.

"It's a gift from Mrs. Whitestone," she said, her chin raised a little too high.

"It is quite nice, madam," he said. He left his eyes on it

instead of returning them to her.

Victoria took a stunted breath in and said in a wavering voice, "I feel…humiliated." She felt an overwhelming emptiness that was like a pitch black cavern inside, and a sudden strange closeness to her butler. She didn't know what she would tell her husband, but she wasn't afraid to say this to a servant. She felt her throat closing up.

"Madam," Collins started when he saw the glassiness of her eyes, "you must only see it as a simple gift from a simple woman."

She noticed that he hadn't expressed any uncertainty over why the birdcage was humiliating. So he had seen it as well. Immediately, he had seen it. A tear dropped unintentionally.

"Is that you, Victoria?" Mr. Hinsley called.

"Into the powder room, madam, you mustn't let anything hurt you this way," he said. "You've come through much worse." He was right. She had. And the fact that her butler would be more caring and understanding than her own husband turned her lone tear to a steady flow.

*

Elizabeth sat for a very long time where Mrs. Hinsley had left her. She'd stared at the couch across from her with nothing, literally nothing going through her mind. It was completely blank. When she'd finally blinked, her eyes were desperate to blink again for moisture. But she continued to stare. She had heard Ashdon come partway into the room before stopping in her tracks, pausing, and leaving quietly. Elizabeth had no idea what she looked like, sitting there staring at nothing, and she didn't have the capacity to imagine.

Mrs. Hinsley had indeed been humiliated. She had

indeed. Yes. And yet nothing in Elizabeth felt settled. Instead she felt dead, like any living roots of feeling had been petrified by this act. She couldn't feel anything. And she had no feelings about that.

At first the blankness was equal to nothingness. Just staring at the couch. But it gently morphed.

When had the affair started between Mrs. Hinsley and Richard? Had it started when Elizabeth was with child? She'd only found out at the baptism with that horrid gift. Elizabeth expelled a puff of air through her nose when she realized: one horrid gift for another horrid gift. Now they were equal. Now Elizabeth was no better.

She thought about what was upstairs. It was not really a baby. It was a thing that existed because of an expectation of marriage. And it wasn't even a boy that could replace Richard as her focus. It was a female, something that bore Mrs. Hinsley's stamp through the baptism gift. It was filthy.

She could do nothing about Mrs. Hinsley if the birdcage didn't deter her. But she could keep this thing upstairs from becoming the next Mrs. Hinsley, the next thing to take Richard away. Richard didn't like it anyway, he didn't want a girl and he didn't like its name. At least Elizabeth was succeeding in one area. And she could continue to succeed. This was all she had now. And she would succeed.

3–4 years old
1843–1844

November 12, 1843

The delicate, scented card arrived at Mrs. Hinsley's home by post, very innocently. Somehow it seemed extra small and delicate like porcelain.

Another baby for the Whitestones.

Another baby for Richard.

Another reminder of her uselessness as a wife, as a woman, even as a mistress. Mr. Hinsley was a patient man, a good man. He considered the Whitestone child his own. The baptism gift hadn't bothered him. After all, it wasn't as if she could carry another man's son. He knew he had her permanently. No other man would take her knowing of her condition. And *everyone* knew of her condition. That's why he was never jealous, never upset, always generous. Arrogant.

Another baby.

Hopefully another failure to produce a boy.

Richard would be livid.

Victoria would pray at church, pray hard, like a good girl, for the wrong thing.

A girl, a girl, a girl, a girl, a girl…

*

Another thing inside her womb. Elizabeth hoped this one didn't have the same oddities about it as Abigail Delilah. She prayed and prayed for a boy over and over again, all day and all night. She didn't hear when Ashdon asked whether she was ready for tea, she seemed to be deaf to Richard's occasional statements and questions. She heard herself constantly saying, "Pardon?" or "What did you say?" She ignored the nursemaid completely. Such stupid questions. No, she didn't want to see Abigail Delilah today. She had more important things to worry about. Like whether this child would be boy.

There was nothing to stop Richard from trying over and over again, except for finally having a son. So she desperately wanted one. This was the only time she wished Mrs. Hinsley wasn't barren. If she could have provided a son that belonged to Richard, Elizabeth may not have had to go through this. But it was not the case. And now all she could do was concentrate hard and hope that it made the difference. Richard seemed to think if she prayed hard enough, she could have a son. He had whispered to her once, "If God thinks it is important enough to you, it will become our miracle." But Elizabeth doubted how that could be possible. Perhaps that very doubt would hinder her ability to create a boy, but she had no faith in the first place that praying for such things could work. Otherwise she would have already had a son last time instead of that wretched thing.

Elizabeth had never felt such worry about something that had so many months to become what it would be. She didn't know how she could live for so long with such worry every day. If this baby wasn't a boy, she would have to do this all over again until she got it right. And that would be a nightmare.

April 2, 1844

The governess took Abigail outside every day now, usually after lunch and before tea, when Mrs. Whitestone was taking her nap. Now that Mrs. Whitestone was six months along, she had to rest as much as possible, especially since she was tired all the time. This baby was taking a lot out of her, but nothing seemed to be wrong. No fever, normal temperatures, no other problems, just a lack of attention to anything going on around her and a constant tiredness.

Sometimes Mrs. Whitestone asked the governess to read to her from the Bible, mostly from Judges, which seemed odd, but she did it anyway. It was hard to tell, but Mrs. Whitestone seemed not only to have very little attention span, but it was almost like she wasn't there at all sometimes. She was completely absent whenever the governess asked if Mrs. Whitestone wanted to see Abigail. She never got a response. After this went on for the first couple of months, the governess stopped asking. She tried to bring in Abigail once, because perhaps Mrs. Whitestone just wasn't relating the name to her current child, as crazy as it seemed. But the governess immediately regretted it. She'd never heard anything like it.

"No, no, no, no, that thing will curse me, get it out of here before it ruins the next child," Mrs. Whitestone had said. The governess knew that if she'd been able to, Mrs. Whitestone probably would have screamed those words. But she was too weak, thank goodness. Instead she was close to tears in the time it took her to say those words, as if she had been long frustrated over the same problem being repeated again and again.

The governess didn't bother anymore, and she hoped desperately that Abigail wouldn't remember that experience. She was only four years old, after all. Perhaps the memory would fade and disappear.

Abigail seemed to respond well to the outside world, finally smiling a little when the governess sat her down on the grass and held up leaves to her and showed her the pretty flowers around the house. She was fascinated by the willow tree though, a tree that was still in its childhood, just like Abigail. The governess would hold Abigail up in front of her and put her just under the young willow's short branches so that she could grab at the strings of leaves, tugging lightly on them. She couldn't get enough of this—it was the only thing that drew a full smile across her face. It was wonderful to see her play with something and enjoy it. The governess made a mental note to take Abigail out here as often as possible for the rest of her time with the Whitestone family. She hoped that Abigail would have at least one purely happy memory of her childhood.

June 1, 1844

Victoria's prayers were answered. Perhaps it was because Mrs. Whitestone didn't go to church anymore. Or perhaps it was punishment for Richard picking the wrong woman to marry. There would be another baptism of course, but Victoria had not been invited this time. Mrs. Whitestone's doing, she was sure. The only way Victoria knew about the baptism was through mutual acquaintances. She hadn't seen Richard since the birth.

This next baby's name was Emma. No second name, no Christian relevance. That couldn't be a coincidence.

She imagined Richard's red ball of hatred for his wife growing rapidly until he would finally do something drastic. It had to happen eventually; something good had to happen for Victoria eventually.

She put her slim index finger through the bars of the birdcage and smiled at her little companion. The canary landed gently on her finger and sat looking around as if it were suddenly in new surroundings.

"Babies don't mean anything, do they?" she said in a honeyed voice. "They don't mean a thing."

June 8, 1844
Richard Whitestone's diary

We will have to try for another child until we get a son. There must be an heir to inherit my fortune and carry on my name. My parents had six girls before I was finally born, and they only rarely went to church. I was sure our obvious loyalty and piousness would break this curse on my family, but it seems Elizabeth is simply not interested in making me happy in any way whatever. Perhaps that is why she has become strange as of late, paranoid and anxious. She barely hears me when I talk, although I haven't spoken to her since she had the latest child. I can at least hope that this one is more normal.

I do not know what sin she committed to beget Abigail, but I will no longer allow the child to suffer for its mother's hateful behaviors, not if I can help it. It would be best to keep Abigail in her room, where her mother will rarely set foot. It would be best for us all.

5–15 years old
1845–1855

February 10, 1845

The first time Abigail saw her mother, she was five years old. It was five years before she was allowed to know who her mother was, what she looked like. And it wasn't a particularly memorable experience. The woman stood in the doorway of Abigail's conservative room, the room of an adult, and stared down at her, not moving forward. It wasn't a mean look, more of an accusatory one. She seemed so extraordinarily tall looking down at Abigail like that.

This was a woman Abigail had seen very little of, one who passed by like a ghost with a mission through the halls. When the nurse-turned-governess said, "Say hi to Mamma," Abigail stared up at this solid, intimidating figure. And it stared back. Abigail said nothing, and then the woman said, "Abigail Delilah is to call me Mother." Abigail called her nothing.

With a sweep of her skirts, the woman turned around and left, her footsteps hard on the wooden floor, deliberate. They had a particular sound to them, those footsteps. Not just a flat *clunk clunk*, but something rounded and always with purpose. Something with forethought. The floorboards never seemed to have any time to creak when she walked on them. Distinct.

When Abigail turned back around to play with her toys, the nurse wore an unmistakably pitying expression.

Abigail smiled. Her eyes didn't.

*

Abigail was instinctively afraid of Mother, the woman always wearing a stern and somewhat angry expression. She was usually either *clunk clunk*ing somewhere in a hurry as if it was somebody's doomsday or she was sitting straight-backed in the parlor's stiff armchair, constantly looking at the door as if she were waiting. Whatever she was waiting for never seemed to come.

Dinner was an intimidating sport with both her parents looming over her, stiff and formal. Neither had anything to say to her. They barely had anything to say to each other. Dinner would be served to them, put on their plates for them, eaten roughly by her mother and oddly quietly by her father, and the most that was said to her was, "You may go," by her mother almost as soon as she'd finished her meal. This wasn't an offer; it was a demand. Abigail found that out when she stayed too long one time, squirming in her seat slightly and trying to say she wanted more food, but before she could get the second word out, her mother reprimanded her.

"Do NOT squirm in your seat or you won't be accepted into better company." Her mother had paused, looking down at her own half-empty plate. Without sparing a glance at Abigail, she'd muttered, "Leave us." When Abigail hesitated, a little frightened to make the wrong move, her mother's cold gaze told her to get out of the chair—now.

These situations didn't bother her too much, aside from the immediate tension and fear. Abigail didn't really think of this woman as her mother. She thought of her as a woman in the house. She tried to forget about her presence altogether in between awkward and intimidating meetings.

Most of Abigail's time was spent in her room or outside

with the governess. The governess had to teach her how to play, with toys and without them. Abigail preferred to sit and look around and think. The governess didn't like this. She said little girls were supposed to play with toys and be carefree. But Abigail didn't feel like a little girl. She would play hopscotch with a straight face, sitting down in the middle of the board when she was done with it. And little dolls didn't interest her. She wanted to try things with them, like taking out strands of their hair and braiding them separate from the dolls, or taking off their clothes and playing just with the clothes. The governess told her she was supposed to play with those things *on* the dolls, not off. But Abigail had no interest in the dolls themselves. Only in what she could keep from them.

May 21, 1845

The governess had half a mind to quit. It was like having her own child, but this wasn't her own child. This was a child whose father didn't want to see her and whose mother was afraid of her. The governess had tried to cover the child's strange under-eye circles with white powder once. When Abigail went in to dinner, her mother gasped. The next thing the governess knew, Mrs. Whitestone had roughly led Abigail into the hall and was grabbing her shoulders, shaking her and saying in a desperate whisper to the governess, "Take it off before it knows why you've done that."

"Madam, I was just trying to—"

"Don't," she said, emphasizing the "t" at the end of the word. Her voice was suddenly hard and sure instead of frightened. "You think it doesn't know what it is? You cannot change it, it's no good and that is what it will always be."

"It will always be," repeated Abigail in her child voice with adult understanding. As if she didn't realized anyone else could see her, she loosened herself from Mrs. Whitestone's grip and walked to the wall, where she pulled braided doll hairs out from between the floorboards and the molding. When the governess looked at Mrs. Whitestone, she was pale, horrified, her slim hand covering a mouth that wanted to scream.

"Abigail, what is that?" she said, a slight quiver in her voice.

Abigail just looked at her.

"Abigail, what have you done?" Angrier, louder this time.

"Madam, she likes to—"

"You let her answer," Mrs. Whitestone sneered.

Abigail looked down at the dark hairs in her small hand. "I don't like them on Dolly. Dolly doesn't need them. She gave them to me because I know what to do with them and she doesn't."

A pause.

"What a peculiar thing to say." Mrs. Whitestone looked down at her daughter with an examining look as if checking a vegetable for rot. "Take her dolls away."

"Madam, I don't think—"

"No one told you to think," Mrs. Whitestone said, each word a carefully pronounced syllable, a carefully pronounced scolding. "If this is what your thinking has done—"

"We both know it's not *my* thinking that has harmed this child."

Mrs. Whitestone's eyes grew to a size that showed the rounding of each eyeball going into its socket. "Get out."

"I will not leave Abigail—"

"GET OUT," she shrieked, her shrill voice echoing through the room.

Mr. Whitestone walked into the hall. "What in God's name is going on here?"

"Look," Abigail's mother said, pointing a trembling hand at the hairs in her daughter's hand. Trembling with anger or trembling with fear, the governess didn't know. "That was pulled out from the floor. Do you see what it does? Pulls out the doll's hair and braids it and hides it around the house!"

"She. Your daughter is a she, not an it," the governess corrected. She made sure to sound patient, unaffected. She held her head high.

Richard's head was in his hand. When he looked up, his hand slid down to cover his mouth. His overwhelming calmness was starting to fail him, the governess could see it.

"Just bring her to her room and put her to bed," Richard said so quietly his words almost went unheard.

"What?" Mrs. Whitestone said, mostly air coming out of her mouth. She left it agape.

"You heard me." He gave the governess a pointed look, turned around and strode quickly out of the room, back to the dining room.

Mrs. Whitestone's mouth remained open, staring after him. Her head pivoted slowly back to the governess, eyes now bloodshot, mouth in a sneer. They looked each other straight in the eye, the governess calm and collected, Mrs. Whitestone almost foaming at the mouth. For the first time, the governess actually felt fear over what Mrs. Whitestone might do. She couldn't show it. She had to remain unaffected.

Mrs. Whitestone took Abigail Delilah's hand roughly.

"Ow!" she squealed. Mrs. Whitestone's knuckles were white. She was squeezing too hard.

"Put it away," she snarled, yanking the child's arm in the governess's direction and letting go. Abigail Delilah lost her balance and fell against the governess, who reached down and lightly grabbed her shoulder to help steady her.

Mrs. Whitestone didn't reappear downstairs again for a week.

July 20, 1845

When the governess turned the corner in the downstairs hallway, she stopped without warning. Abigail sat with her knees to her chest, each hand wrapped around a shin, head leaning heavily against the enormous grandfather clock. Her eyes were squeezed shut, intent with concentration.

The governess didn't want to disturb her; this looked like a very rare peaceful moment alone that seemed to matter to the girl, a very rare and necessary moment. But if Mrs. Whitestone happened into the hallway…

"Abig—"

"Shhh," the child said gently. "Wait."

The governess waited, though she didn't know for what. She looked at the clock. The minute hand was nearing the hour. As soon as it struck the sixtieth second of the minute, Abigail opened her eyes, breathed in deeply, and let out a heavy, long breath. She looked at the clock intimately and ran her hands down its smooth, dark wood finish until her fingers hit the molding and hung there as if hanging onto something she could fall off of, as if her whole body weight depended on those fingertips' strength. Abigail's fascination lay not with the detailed carvings of flowers on the front, the intricate patterns and careful work, but with the smooth side of the clock, the flat side.

"Thank you, Governess," she said somewhat shyly, relief evident in her tone. She still looked at the clock.

"What were you doing, if you don't mind my asking?" the governess said.

"Listening to the clock," Abigail responded as if it made perfect sense. She ran her fingers along the molding, her eyes following them.

"Can you tell me why?" the governess asked.

Abigail's big blue eyes met the governess's. One finger tapped on the hollow side of the clock, loud and in time. "Because I can hear its heartbeat." The child's tired eyes looked back at the clock. "Mother never had a heartbeat." The governess almost wept.

Abigail thought Emma was rather lovely, pink cheeked and always making sweet sounds. She had finally been introduced to the baby by the governess when Emma was one year old. The governess had even let her hold the baby, keeping her arms below Abigail's as a precaution. She liked holding it. Its warmth, its blue eyes, its silly little bird mouth. She loved it.

When the governess first told Abigail about the baby when she was first born, she'd said Emma had a special room with everything it needed, and now Abigail would have to expect to see less of her caretaker because the baby needed a lot of attention.

"It doesn't mean I love you any less," the governess had said. "And I'll make sure our time together counts. We'll do everything you like to do." And she kept her promise. She made sure Abigail had lots to do on her own, and when the governess spent time with her, Abigail dictated what they did. She was becoming very interested in nature, but of course they couldn't go outside because the governess didn't have time. Instead the governess brought her leaves and grass and dirt to play with.

"This has to be our special secret," the governess said. "Your mother wouldn't approve. Do you understand?"

Abigail understood. She understood Mother was something not to be trifled with. She understood there would be consequences to any behavior Mother deemed unacceptable, which could be anything at any given moment. So Abigail hid her nature. She hid it inside the dolls she'd already cut the hair off of, ones the governess had let her keep despite Mother's orders to eliminate all dolls from her room. Abigail cut the threads that bound the bisque head, neck, and shoulders to their bodies with sewing scissors she'd snuck out of the governess's room. Then she stored groupings of all her nature in each doll's head: a little grass, some dirt, and a couple of leaves in each one. She wanted to be fair and let them all have some. That was the right thing to do. She would have adored the addition of a flower to each one, but she was grateful to have anything at all. After she was satisfied and she thought her doll was also satisfied with the secret it now held, she put it back in her toy chest and sat the bisque carefully atop the soft body so it would look like nothing was wrong. She wasn't old enough to have a sewing kit yet. The scissors she'd taken were most important anyway.

As Abigail was picking up a doll from the chest, she didn't hold the bisque top on tightly enough and it clattered to the floor. The head shattered into four uneven pieces, but the shoulders stayed intact. Panicky, Abigail gathered the pieces; then an idea suddenly struck her. One at a time, she put a broken piece inside each of the other dolls she'd already cut open. Perhaps they would be just like seeds and another doll would grow from each of them. Perhaps she could have her own baby now, one that was just like Emma, and she could hold its warmth in her arms forever. She thought about Emma for a moment. It had been a long time since she'd seen Emma now. It would be so nice to give her a present.

*

It took a long time for Abigail's wounds to heal after Mother found the broken doll and dirt in Emma's crib and slashed her nails into Abigail's throat. The governess had heard Mother's wild shriek and made it just in time to stop

Mother from digging her nails in again.

Abigail had learned one thing.

If Mother had found the doll in Emma's crib the morning after Abigail had left it there, that meant Mother visited Emma more often than Abigail.

Abigail had learned one other thing.

The governess would defend her no matter what.

August 17, 1845
Richard Whitestone's diary

I try my best to keep Elizabeth civil toward Abigail. Most of the time Elizabeth leaves her be, although she lacks the warmth a mother should have. It is such a shame I did not ask the correct woman to be my wife.

Over the past couple of days, I have noticed that Abigail has been wearing high-necked dresses and scarves even though it is not yet cold enough for those fashions. I could not get a straight answer from the governess as to why, but when I entered Abigail's room alone, I lowered the neck of her dress and found wide, deep scratch marks that looked recent. And then I remembered. The governess had threatened to quit, "If the abuse continued," she had said. Those were her exact words. She had not expanded further on her point. She had also made sure to tell me when I was alone. I had thought perhaps Elizabeth was being unkind to the governess, but I was horribly mistaken.

Elizabeth has gone too far this time. She will have to pay a price for her actions now. I have never disciplined her before, but I have no choice now.

September 21, 1845

Abigail considered herself fortunate that Mother was having a difficult pregnancy. She didn't know what it meant, but she knew Mother didn't come to the table for meals anymore, which meant there was no thinly veiled anger causing Abigail's stomach to reject her food. Mother didn't come downstairs at all anymore, leaving Abigail free to walk around without fear of upsetting Mother for reasons she never understood. Mother hadn't even come outside her room in a couple of months, so Abigail could leave her bedroom door open instead of constantly being shut inside.

Father didn't mention anything about Mother's condition, but the governess said Mother had trouble moving without pain. Abigail did feel sorry for that, but she also felt that whatever kept Mother away couldn't be such a bad thing.

Of course Mother didn't want to see Abigail and Abigail didn't want to see Mother. Emma was taken into Mother's room, though, in her little white dresses. Sometimes she would be in there for half the day. The governess said Emma made Mother feel better. Abigail wished Emma made *her* feel better too, because even though she was happy not to be living in fear, it was an empty happiness, a hollowness she couldn't explain. There was a deep black pit inside her that somehow she hadn't noticed before Mother had withdrawn herself into her room. It was confusing and Abigail couldn't grasp what it meant or why it was there.

It helped when the governess was around, but that wasn't very often anymore, now that she had both Emma and Mother to take care of. Abigail had taken to wandering around outside on her own, at first scared to step out the door without an adult, but she became more and more bold until she felt she could take care of herself. She was only on the property, she hadn't gone outside it, but still, she felt a slight bit of something foreign. She felt she knew something others didn't, that she could handle something others didn't think she could. It made her heart feel whole and it put a bandage over the black emptiness she couldn't identify.

Abigail realized that she could find her own nature outside and bring it in for herself instead of waiting for the governess to retrieve it. And this was the best discovery of all. But she had to think ahead. She had to store it up for the future. After Mother was walking around again, Abigail most likely would no longer be able to walk free. But how would she store it? She could take something from the kitchen to collect it in, but where would she put it? And wouldn't the cook miss whatever she took?

No, she had to be clever.

She went to her room and sorted through some of the toys in her chest, toys the governess had bought her and that she treasured for that reason. She tore a jack out of her jack-in-the-box and used the teapot from her little tea set. In one she could pack dirt and in the other she could carefully store leaves. If she could fit a flower or two she would, but they were very delicate and required special handling.

She would have to fix her own problems from now on, and this was how she would start.

December 5, 1845

Abigail was sitting by the grandfather clock while she listened to Mother's incredibly loud screams. The governess said the new baby was coming, but Abigail didn't remember this happening when Emma came. There were two people, a woman and a man she had never seen before to help with the coming of the baby.

In her usual position with her knees to her chest, Abigail pressed her ear to the clock and tried to concentrate on its rhythmic *tick tock tick tock*, but she couldn't drown out the horrible sounds from upstairs.

Father was in the parlor, waiting. He sat with his elbows on his knees and his fists holding his head up, a completely abnormal posture for him. He was usually stock straight. Every once in a while he would run his hand down his face and resume his position.

Abigail knew better than to talk to him when he was like this. She had tried to talk to him when Emma was coming, and he had shooed her away with a dismissive flick of his hands, a deep frown on his face. This time was much worse what with the yelling echoing through the house, so Abigail knew not to bother him. She wondered how Emma felt, still being a baby. Was she frightened? Abigail was a little frightened, so Emma must have been terrified.

Abigail heard the clock gong midnight. Mother had been making the baby for ten hours now. Emma had not taken that long. Why couldn't Mother make it faster?

More time passed, and when the screams had stopped for more than ten minutes, Father ran upstairs, taking them two at a time. Abigail wondered if she had caused all this fuss when she was made. She doubted it. She wondered what a baby would be like that caused all this fuss.

Heavy, fast steps down the stairs made Abigail look up to see Father bounding down.

"Abigail, Abigail," he said in a tone new to her, "you have a baby brother!"

December 6, 1845
Richard Whitestone's diary

I finally have a son. It has taken so long—nine years since our marriage—but finally it has been done. Elizabeth has suffered greatly to deliver this boy to me, and I firmly believe she finally atoned for the sins that prevented this miracle before. Perhaps now she will become a kinder mother to Abigail, and she will become a better wife. This could make all the difference to us.

December 19, 1845

Victoria peered at the varieties of birdseed she had lined up in front of the canary's cage. She had bought almost every single kind now, including little treats. Her bird was spoiled like her child would have been, and she loved it. Every time she bought something new for it, she felt a rush of happiness and couldn't wait to take it home and see if her little birdie liked it. It invariably did and her smile grew wider every time.

Richard finally had his son now. He had what he wanted from his wife. What this meant for their relationship, Victoria had no idea. She had heard about the son through other people, not from Richard himself. She hadn't received a letter or a visit from him since the birth. What would her life would become without him? Her bird was all she had left that mattered to her anymore. Society and her own home fell far short now that she had experienced what it felt like to be loved genuinely by a man, and not just because he knew he could easily keep her. Her social life was still active, but she just didn't care much for it anymore. And she was a good enough actress with her husband. He had never complained. But bouts of severe sadness overwhelmed her at random times that sometimes kept her from going out of the house. She just needed to hear from him…

The birdie tweeted and chirped, and Victoria smiled weakly.

"You're my little baby," she said softly to it. "You understand me." The clawing need continued unbroken. She realized her self-validation lay in Richard's hands and she hated that, but she didn't hate it enough to stop it. And perhaps she was being too extreme in the first place. She needed to give him time to be with his son before he had time for Victoria.

She had this internal conversation with herself every day, and every day she grew more and more sick of herself. He had to come back to church eventually, and that was the only thing that kept her going.

May 26, 1849

How can a woman ever forget the reason her husband beats her? She cannot. She could never. It is true that provoking him is wrong after she knows what causes it, but sometimes a woman can toe the line. Especially if she is beaten in favor of her competition.

Elizabeth put her hand over Emma's smaller one. "Are you still hungry? Do you want some more?" she asked in a sickening baby voice. She hated the sound of it herself, but she couldn't stop.

Emma had a beautiful smile and a perfect face with curls of strawberry blond hair that fell perfectly around it. She was a normal child who spoke her little disjointed words in a way that suited her age and she played in normal ways, although she hated dolls for some reason. Perhaps it was what that dreadful other one had done to her when she was only one year old.

Abigail sat on Elizabeth's other side and watched Elizabeth make a spectacle of paying too much attention to Emma, who ate it up.

"Would you like something sweet?" Elizabeth asked Emma in that same awful baby voice.

"She's too young for sweets," Richard said in his monotone drone.

"Nonsense, she can have anything she wants," she said to him. "You can have any," Elizabeth touched Emma's nose with her forefinger, "thing," now it moved to her chin, "you want," and finally pinched her cheek gently.

"That's enough," Richard said, sounding agitated. "Abigail, if you're finished you can go."

Abigail left the table without a word.

"In fact I feel sick myself," Richard said. "Good night."
Elizabeth's rubber band smile quickly fell away once Richard was gone.

"Can I sweet?" Emma asked, still all smiles.

"No," Elizabeth said bluntly and picked her up to put her away in her room.

*

It was nearly midnight when Abigail crept out of her room and eased the door next to hers open. Emma was asleep in her small bed. Abigail walked very slowly and quietly to the bed and stood over her sister. Emma was sleeping on her side, facing away from Abigail, and her covers had come up so that they were only covering the front of her body.

Abigail crouched next to the bed and took out her needle that was already threaded, something the governess had been using to teach her to embroider. She had already tied a knot at the end of the thread; she had been well prepared. Taking a small bit of Emma's long nightgown that was laying outside of the covers, Abigail carefully put the needle through the gathered bit of cloth. Then she brought the only full, whole doll she had onto the bed and placed it with such care upon the mattress that she didn't even hear or feel any effect from it. She sewed the front of the doll's dress onto the back of Emma's nightgown and made sure it wouldn't come loose. Then she cut the thread and drew her hands away slowly. She took the needle and thread and crept back out of the room.

Abigail knew she would be beaten for it, but she couldn't help herself. She felt driven to attach something Emma hated to her, just like Abigail was attached to Mother. It was not by choice. It was by misfortune. And

Abigail was determined not to be the only one to suffer.

*

Emma awoke early in the morning when she turned over in bed. She felt something pulling at the bottom of her nightgown. She pulled the sheets out and up, but something still pulled. She threw back the covers and saw...hair? In her sleepy state it took her a moment to realize how out of place it was. She snapped out of it quickly and gasped, sitting up, and the hair followed her movement. She opened her mouth, unsure whether to scream. She moved away from it, but it followed her. Now she saw a body attached to the hair, a small body that kept following her. She jumped out of bed, away from the thing and felt it hit her leg. She screamed, running to her door, trying to get away, but she felt it banging against her leg as she ran. What if it was alive? What if it hurt her? What if it could climb her dress all the way up to her face and... She threw open her door and ran for her parents' bedroom, but before she could make it there the governess grabbed hold of her shoulders and stopped her.

"What is it?" she asked, looking exhausted. But Emma couldn't speak. She screamed again, afraid the little person or monster on her dress was climbing further onto her as she stood there. She grabbed at her nightgown and jerked it up and down, hoping to make the thing fall off, but she still felt the weight of it hanging on.

"What? What?" the governess asked, frantic now.

Mother ran out of her room and knelt behind Emma. She felt Mother tug at the thing clinging to her nightgown, and when she couldn't get it off, Mother held it up to show Emma. A doll. It must have been alive, it must have grabbed onto her, it wanted to hurt her, just like the last one that was just a head. Emma screamed louder. She didn't take another conscious breath after that. Mother's face blurred, the doll in front of it still sharply in focus, and then blackness.

*

Screaming woke Abigail up, screaming from the next room. Emma's room. Abigail kept her eyes closed and smiled a little. She'd gotten Emma good. Though part of her took pleasure in disrupting Emma's perfect life, part of her started hurting. It was wrong, it was, and she knew it, but it was right too, wasn't it? *It feels bad because I know I'll get punished for it, but it was right, it was right.* She flipped onto her side away from the door, squeezed her eyes tight, and covered her face with her blankets, waiting for someone to come in and yell at her and worse.

But nobody came in after Emma stopped screaming, and Abigail was too afraid to go out. Her heart pounded harder after the screaming stopped than while it was going on. *Spoiled, spoiled*, she tried to convince herself of her sister, but regret had already seeped in and she began to cry a little. Just a couple of hot tears running down her nose and onto the pillow.

How long could she stay there? When would they come get her? Should she go out on her own? What would she say? It was too late to go out and ask what happened. She had taken too long for that. Now she would be in real trouble. *Bad, bad, bad, stupid, stupid, should have thought it through better.* She should have run out when Emma first started screaming to seem like she wanted to help, like she was concerned. Now it was obvious she had done something wrong. No, better yet, she shouldn't have done something so obvious as sewing something to her sister's nightgown. There was nobody else in the house to blame for it. They knew it was her already. But then why was it taking so long for someone to come in?

She was going crazy with fear and worry when she heard a click at the door. It wasn't the click of the door opening, though. It was the click of the door locking from the outside. Abigail froze. She was too afraid to even think in case someone heard her thoughts. She waited for what seemed like 20 minutes but it was probably just one. She wanted to try the doorknob, but what if someone heard her trying to open it? What could happen? She had no idea. And not knowing was the scariest thing of all.

It has been more than 24 hours since Elizabeth locked Abigail in her room without a word to her. It would have been better to have just punished her when the incident first happened, but this…this is inhuman. I have asked her for the key, I've told her how cruel it is, regardless of what Abigail did. I've told her why Abigail must have done it, because Elizabeth bred jealousy and hatred in her own nine-year-old daughter, but she won't hear it. I shook her hard, rattled her, I couldn't stop myself, she is so unreasonable, but no amount of threats or hurt will make her give me the key to Abigail's room. I cannot figure out what she has done with it. I even threw her into a chair and checked the pockets in her dress, but it wasn't there and she took the greatest, most insane pleasure in telling me I would never find it.

I cannot talk to Abigail through the door. What would I say? That I cannot unlock it? That only Mother has the key? That I am impotent when it comes to that woman? Elizabeth will always get her way with anything in this house, no matter what I do to her. She is insane. I must get rid of her, she is destroying Abigail. But first I must find the key. Only God knows the damage this has done to Abigail. Although I fear all of our futures may suffer for it.

*

Elizabeth waited until Richard was out of the house. He had threatened to get a locksmith since the key he had for Abigail's room no longer worked. He was absolutely livid when he realized Elizabeth had changed the lock without telling him. When that had happened, he'd never know.

Now he literally ran to get the locksmith. She knew he had more in mind, too, but Elizabeth already knew what to do about it. The governess was taking care of Christopher two doors down from Abigail.

Very quietly, Elizabeth unlocked Abigail's door and eased it open slowly, stepped inside, and closed the door behind her. Abigail was sitting in the corner of her room, her knees pulled up to her chest, her arms around them. The dark circles under her eyes had become darker, and her face looked even more pale than usual.

"Be very quiet," Elizabeth said softly. "I'm going to let you out of this room."

Abigail said nothing, just hugged her knees tighter to her chest. She seemed afraid. Good.

Elizabeth reached into her pocket and took out a steak knife. "Do you see this?"

Abigail didn't seem sure whether the question was rhetorical, but at Elizabeth's pause for an answer, Abigail nodded gently.

"Do you know what it does?" Elizabeth asked.

Abigail nodded again.

"It cuts through meat," Elizabeth said, "and it hurts very badly." She pointed the knife at Abigail. "You will be a good girl now. You will always be a good girl now. Always. Do I have to explain what happens if you're not a good girl?"

Abigail shook her head hard.

"Good." Elizabeth put the knife back into her side slit pocket. "Father will be back soon with a man. You weren't in this room for more than an hour, were you?"

Abigail stared and frowned a little. When Elizabeth put her hand back into her pocket, Abigail squeaked out, "No."

Elizabeth took her hand back out empty. "Address me."

"No, Mother," Abigail said, barely audible.

"That's a good girl." Elizabeth left the room and as she reached the steps, she heard the front door open.

"Up here," she heard Richard say.

She didn't know what to do with herself and ended up just standing in the hallway at the top of the stairs.

Richard bounded up the steps, a man behind him, and when she didn't move out of his way, he pushed her aside with the back of his hand to her waist. When he and the locksmith reached Abigail's open door, the locksmith right behind him, he stopped short.

"Elizabeth," he said, turning around. His eyes were red. "You are trying my patience. How dare you wait until I leave the house to open this door after all you've put me through. Me and your own daughter. How dare you make me look like a fool." He turned to the locksmith. "She's playing games, I told you this door was locked and it was." Then he looked into the room at Abigail, who stood by her bed now, looking awful. "Abigail, tell the man how long you've been locked in here."

Abigail froze. Elizabeth silently walked behind Richard so that Abigail could see her and patted her dress pocket.

"Abigail," Richard said, "tell the locksmith what happened."

Abigail didn't move.

"I'm sorry he's wasted your time," Elizabeth said to the locksmith. "Sometimes I think his nerves are getting worse."

"Don't make a fool of me, Elizabeth," Richard threatened. "You know what you did. Abigail, don't be afraid of her. Tell the man what happened."

Abigail stuttered, "I-I did something bad and-and I was locked in my room for an hour."

Richard stared at her with his mouth open. "Abigail." He quickly turned to Elizabeth and saw her pointed stare directed at Abigail. His mouth closed as realization hit. "I see." Elizabeth did not look at him. "It seems I've wasted your time," he said to the locksmith, still looking at Elizabeth. "Thank you very much for coming. Can you show yourself out?" Richard reached into his pocket and handed the man some money without counting it.

"Thank you, sir," the locksmith said and left without asking any questions.

When the front door closed behind him, Richard took a step toward Elizabeth. "What did you say to Abigail," he said without a question in his voice.

"Never mind," she said in a low, thin voice he'd never heard before. "She will be a good girl from now on."

Richard stared at her. "You have no conscience, do you? There isn't even a fraction of an ounce of God left in you."

Elizabeth stared back. "God did not save me from you and He will not save her from me," she said and walked past him.

June 17, 1854

Abigail, Emma, Christopher, and Father arrived at church early enough to sit in their usual pew without having to squeeze by anyone. Father hated getting there late, and it rarely ever happened. Abigail only remembered one single time they'd gotten to church late, and it was because of Mother and her refusal to go. Father and Abigail ended up leaving without her and getting there late. Not wanting to be rude and squeeze through the packed pew, they'd sat elsewhere. Father didn't speak to Mother at dinner that night, which wasn't very different from any other night, except the feeling in the air between them was more than just sour. It was malicious, as if there were sharp teeth hovering between them that threatened to bite.

Mother hadn't come to church since.

Abigail would sit and stand and sit and stand in church every Sunday between Mrs. Hinsley and Emma, until Emma and Christopher went off to Sunday school. Then she sat between Mrs. Hinsley and Father, which was quite nice. She was glad Father had decided they would sit next to the Hinsleys once Mother stopped coming to church all that time ago.

If Abigail got lost trying to find the correct hymn to sing, Mrs. Hinsley would help her turn the pages and point to the words as they were sung. Mrs. Hinsley would smile at her and sometimes even pat her back when the minister read passages, not looking up from the Bible in his pulpit. Abigail did not completely understand all the passages, but she tried to concentrate on them, hoping that at some point God would reveal their meaning to her.

Once she asked her old Sunday school teacher what

something the minister had read meant. She'd kept her finger on the spot throughout the sermon and waited until Emma and Christopher had gone out to meet Father. It was Ecclesiastes 4:1–3. "So I returned, and considered all the oppressions that are done under the sun: and behold the tears of such as were oppressed, and they had no comforter; and on the side of their oppressors there was power; but they had no comforter," she read out loud, slowly but without stumbling. "Wherefore I praised the dead which are already dead more than the living which are yet alive. Yea, better than both they, which hath not yet been, who hath not seen the evil work that is done under the sun."

The Sunday school teacher looked at Abigail, surprised that this was the passage the child wanted to understand.

"Wouldn't you like to know what the whole story is about?" she asked sweetly. Perhaps the child would dedicate herself to the church when she grew older. If the rumors about her and her family were true, she would benefit from making God her future.

Abigail shook her head. "Just that section," she said.

Looking at the child instead of the book, the teacher said, "Well, out of context it's a bit...a bit dark, Abigail."

Abigail waited, undeterred, with a wide-eyed stare that was hard to endure. The teacher looked back down at the Bible.

"Those particular verses are just the beginning of the whole section, but they say that people who are dead or who have not yet been born are better off than those who are living but held down by another—those who are oppressed," she said, running her finger over the final word and then looking back up at the child.

At first Abigail did not react, but beneath her

unblinking eyes and her steady chin, the Sunday school teacher saw Abigail swallow.

"But remember," the teacher said more loudly and more suddenly than intended, "that is only *part* of —"

"Thank you," Abigail said and turned around abruptly to leave.

"Abigail, that isn't the whole—"

But Abigail had already run off.

July 1, 1855

Abigail, Emma, Christopher, and Father still went to church, unlike Mother, who seemed to stay in bed every Sunday morning when it was time to leave. Abigail loved the feeling of being cleansed in the house of God, of being unafraid for just a couple of hours. She liked to think of it as a lot of minutes all piled up into a well-earned time of newness; that was how she always felt after church: new. That feeling could melt away quickly at home, depending on what Mother's mood was, but Abigail soaked up her new feeling while she had it. She waited for that time once a week, impatient, and sometimes when she felt the mild relief of lying in bed at night—the tension lessened but not completely gone—she pictured herself in church. She had to squeeze her eyes hard, and she still couldn't get quite the same feeling, but she could picture it well enough and she could picture herself in it. Sometimes she pictured other people, too, but mostly just her and the minister and his pulpit and the organ and the expanse between herself and the pulpit. It seemed such a large distance. A distance with enough depth to cast shadows.

Trying to conjure the image of the church or the minister—a cardboard, white-haired cutout with an internal glow, in Abigail's head—was impossible while she was anywhere but in bed. It was her only place of safety, of aloneness. Anywhere else could lead Mother to confront her with harsh moods that rippled ahead of her before she said anything to Abigail. It was impossible to focus on church when Abigail wasn't in bed. So she counted down the hours to bed and the minutes to church.

Years ago, before Emma and Christopher were old

enough to attend church, she had made excuses to stop going to Sunday school. "I don't feel well, Father" or "I'm scared of the teacher, Father" or "It's so cold in that room, Father, don't make me go." At first, Father had been very hesitant and uncomfortable. He didn't seem to like the idea, judging by the way he had shifted back and forth in his seat or on his feet. But somehow she'd gotten away with it and she made sure she was well behaved so he wouldn't change his mind. The next couple of times he'd become less certain, probably discovering her pattern, but Mrs. Hinsley had leaned around Abigail and whispered to Father, and Abigail soon found she was allowed to stay without making excuses. So she remained with the adults and Mrs. Hinsley continued to pat her back sometimes. As long as Abigail was a good girl, she seemed to consistently avoid Sunday school. And when Mother forced Father to start bringing Emma to church, and then Christopher, Abigail sat at the end of the pew so that she could take the children out if either started to cry. Father didn't like where Abigail sat, but Mrs. Hinsley had a word and Father seemed to forget his opposition to it. Abigail was very attentive to her siblings, taking them outside any time they made noise. If Abigail stayed out of Father's way, she stood even less of a chance of being sent to Sunday school. So why not?

Abigail often forgot that Mr. Hinsley was there. He stood on the left side of his wife and he didn't speak to Father during the service. He was a handsome man, Abigail noticed, nicely groomed, like Father. He was about the same height as Mrs. Hinsley, so she couldn't even see him past her figure as she sat and stood. Abigail would feel an extra hard thump of her heart when he would appear after the service because she always completely forgot about him, as if he were a blank spot in her brain that shocked her into remembering his existence. He would shake hands with Father after the service and they would always say the same thing:

"Good morning, Mr. Whitestone," Mr. Hinsley would say brightly.

"Good morning, Mr. Hinsley," Father would say more conservatively. "How are you?" His voice was always a bit lower when speaking to Mr. Hinsley, a bit more reserved, somehow duller.

"Quite well, thank you. You're looking well yourself." How come Mr. Hinsley always smiled broadly and Father didn't?

Father nodded, looking down at the ground. Why wasn't there eye contact at that point? A response? Abigail always wanted to respond for Father, "Oh thank you, I am", or even, "Yes, right." She was embarrassed at his silence, at his examination of the ground. It was something that made her feel uncomfortable inside, like some of her organs had rearranged themselves.

That was usually about as far as their conversations went.

At that point, after a slightly extended moment of awkward silence, Mrs. Hinsley would step forward, her skirts swinging. They always swung with the suddenness of this same exact movement every week, and Abigail could always hear them above any noise around her, whether it be conversations or buzzing bees or her own mind working too fast. She wished she could feel the skirts brush her, that she was next to Mrs. Hinsley, close to her. She imagined they would feel velvety against her arm, regardless of the fabric. Velvety soft.

"Please say hello to Mrs. Whitestone for me," Mrs. Hinsley would say to Father, smiling pearls of teeth. Her teeth seemed no different than Mother's, and yet they did look different. To Abigail, Mrs. Hinsley would say, "And you take care, Miss Whitestone. You be a good young lady for your father."

Not "for your mother," Abigail noticed. "For your father." Always.

Then the Hinsleys would leave, and Abigail and Father would stand in the same spot for a few moments, people passing by and acknowledging Father, Father mustering a small smile or a nod of the head. Abigail watched him and it was always the same. An unfinished feeling like reading a good book and not reaching the end even though you wanted to.

Always the same.

It seemed an odd place to loiter, outside a church. Why not stay inside, where they would still be in the spirit of holiness, and say goodbye to the Hinsleys? Why go outside right away? This became an even more pressing question for Abigail when it was winter and the icy wind numbed her face. First her ears, then her nose, and her cheeks would burn, but there Father stood, in the wake of departure. They would only leave once almost everyone else had left. Abigail had only tried tugging on his coat once or twice, but he had no reaction, and she hated to be a nuisance to him. She kept her brother and sister in line, squeezing their hands a little too tight and giving them harsh looks that probably scared them. But this was clearly how it was supposed to be for him. And so it would be for her and her siblings, too. So in the winter she would bob lightly against the cold, encouraging Emma and Christopher to do the same, and in the summer they would all stand stark still, as if the less movement they made, the faster they might leave. She knew this wasn't the case, but it seemed she should leave him alone and let him be. It seemed abhorrent to disturb his silence.

In time, Emma and Christopher both began wandering off to speak to other people as they developed friendships. They both went to Sunday school and seemed to like it better than the sermons; neither ever tried to escape like Abigail had. Abigail, however, learned both patience and ritual in standing by Father, until such things became natural, though even at that point she always noticed each second as it ticked by. The only difference was that she accepted it more and more as she aged, as a part of life, something unavoidable. Quite like age itself. Unavoidable and perpetual.

16–19 years old
1856–1859

October 10, 1856
Richard Whitestone's diary

I gave Abigail my old Bible that Elizabeth used to read. Elizabeth no longer uses it nor does she attend church, which is really no surprise. I did not tell Abigail that Elizabeth used to use it or else she probably would not have taken it.

I just hope she reads it closely and finds something that could make her right. I do not know what else to do for her. She seems to want to come to church, and yet she is always more than willing to take the other children outside when they balk. She must choose to leave for a reason, but I haven't the courage to force her to stay.

She accepted the Holy Book with shaking hands that I held in my own for a moment. She was unable to speak. I thought perhaps I could break whatever lives inside her that causes Elizabeth to treat her so badly. I shall continue to pray for her soul.

October 12, 1859

Abigail wandered across the grounds of Father's property, carrying her book and treading slowly through still green grass. Leaves of fall, red and brown and even some yellow, crunched under her feet. She liked to kick them up as she walked. It was chilly, but she'd refused a jacket. She liked the chill. And the crunch of the dead leaves underfoot felt more like home than the creaking of the wood floors in the house. Those wood floors…always giving everyone away, always with some small space in between or knot-turned-hole. There could be anything under there and no one would ever know it. There could be lost jewelry. Perhaps a soul or two. Perhaps that's where Mother's soul went. It seeped down from her feet, between the floorboards while she ascended in her typical foul mood one evening. It didn't want to be with her either.

Abigail thought how nice it would be without Mother. Just Father, the governess, and her brother…and her sister. Just the five of them. That would be nice.

The single weeping willow on the property was her favorite place to go. Upon sight it made her happy, a place of beautiful escape. It was a brilliant green, gemstone green, with wispy, long streams of oblong leaves that hung gracefully from wavy dark brown branches. She and the tree had grown up together; now that it was also nineteen years old, its leaves touched the ground almost all the way around, sparse in places and thick in others. She ran her fingers through the strands of leaves like hair, sliding them straight down, then twirling them around. Finally she parted them and went through. Inside was a dim, even cooler, fresh world of closed-in comfort. It always felt as though no one could see her here, as if it were a room with a door and she could lock herself in. Little bits of light could stream in here and there, but for the most part, it was quite a bit darker than the shining outside world. What made the sky so bright anyway? Was there so much to show out there? No, not for her. It was much better to see less and appreciate what little she had. It was much better to find comfort in what she could keep, what she knew was hers.

Walking to the trunk of the weeping willow, Abigail heard a breeze against the leaves but felt nothing. That made her smile. She sat down against the tree sideways, leaning her shoulder against the trunk. She opened the Bible in her arms.

Mother came to mind, how she'd always said she had a headache, and she didn't even bother saying *that* anymore to escape church attendance. If she was out of the bedroom before Father and Abigail left with the children, she would just touch her head with her forefinger, middle finger, and thumb, letting her other fingers dangle.

The little ones loved church. They always smiled, and sometimes they got a bit rowdy. Abigail would take one or both of them outside when this happened until they calmed down. She insisted on taking them.

She wanted to.

The Bible was heavy with lessons yet simple in appearance, just brown leather with an unbending cover. The most ornate thing about it was the words "Holy Bible" printed along the side in gold and the beautiful gilt of the pages. It did not have color printing on the inside, something that was quite frivolous in Abigail's opinion anyway. It took attention away from the words. No, this was the most beautiful version in existence.

Mother had accused her of stealing it when she first started carrying it around the house with her, Mother's bunched up, angry features hovering over her while she accused and accused. She hadn't stolen it. Father had bought it for her and lain it in her hands almost exactly three years ago, tenderly closing his own around hers. He had half smiled. That was the most wonderful moment she had ever experienced from either of her parents. Her heart had overflowed with the recognition of a truly loving act, a gift she now held dear.

She'd learned long ago that things that made her happy made Mother angry, and anything having to do with Father seemed to make her angrier, especially since he sometimes helped Abigail escape Mother's wrath. Abigail couldn't tell Mother the Bible was a gift from Father, so she said her Sunday school teacher gave it to her for being such a good student. It was strange, how quiet Mother had gotten at that. The bunching of her face came undone, and what was left was a furrowed brow and squinting eyes. Mother had backed away then, as if Abigail had threatened her with holy water and Mother wasn't sure if the threat was real. Then Mother had retreated, just turned around, her dress billowing a bit, and ran up the stairs. Really ran.

Abigail had received the Bible from Father only three years ago, but already the cover was worn from her constant use of it, if not to read it then to feel its solid strength beneath her fingertips, on her palms, in her arms. She smiled with the memory of Father's half smile, the only occasion of his touch, and she flipped in her Bible to Psalm 58:10. "The righteous shall rejoice when he seeth the vengeance: he shall wash his feet in the blood of the wicked."

That section comforted her the most.

*

Elizabeth had not believed that the Sunday school teacher had given a Bible to that shadowy creature with its pale, tired face, constantly working things out, thinking what to say, what *not* to say. The only way that could be true was if the Sunday school teacher had the same exact understanding of this child that Elizabeth did.

Elizabeth would speak with her immediately.

October 14, 1856

It would take Abigail even longer to get over this beating than the scratches Mother had dug into her when she'd put the doll head in Emma's bed eleven years ago. She had been beaten all over her body with the Bible she loved so much. She could feel the bruising, but she couldn't see it yet. She had been afraid to fight back. What if Mother beat her worse? Or cut her? Or broke one of her bones? There was always worse that could happen... She had been on the floor by the time she admitted Father had given her the Bible, whimpering the words in a squeaky, high-pitched voice she was ashamed of. Mother got even angrier after that, but after one last hard hit to Abigail's thigh, Mother finally left the room. She didn't even bother to close the door.

The governess had been out shopping; Emma and Christopher had been out visiting. Which probably meant Mother had waited until they were gone to avoid any interference. Her brother and sister probably wouldn't have done anything, but the governess had defended her before. Was Mother...could she be...afraid of the governess? Perhaps she was afraid the governess would take Abigail away.

Abigail propped her chin up on her hand, her elbow against the floor. If Mother was afraid of losing Abigail, perhaps Mother needed her after all. Perhaps Mother just didn't understand Abigail, and that was why she beat her and avoided her. Perhaps if Abigail could be more like Mother, they'd understand each other better.

Very interesting.

October 14, 1856
Richard Whitestone's diary

I returned home today to find the governess's room empty. Only a note remained on her writing desk, scribbled angrily:

> Mr. Whitestone,
> Ask Abigail how she is feeling. I hope she recovers quickly. I hope I will too.

She hadn't even signed it. Dumbfounded, I knocked on Abigail's door and was greeted by just one eye peeking out of the barely open door.

"Abigail, do you know what this means?" I asked, and I slipped the paper through to her. I didn't want to ask her to open the door further; it was such odd behavior in the first place. She stuck her head out and looked both ways down the hallway. I didn't know at the time what she was looking for, but in retrospect, it must have been Elizabeth. I wonder how many times a day she looks out of her room in just that manner. I feel such hatred flood my senses when I realize how this child's life is lived.

She opened the door wider and let me in but closed the door so quickly behind me, she could have caught my jacket.

"The governess is gone," Abigail said, but she didn't elaborate.

"And why is that?" I asked. Abigail just stared back at me. I repeated my question, then added, "And why does she say she hopes you recover quickly? Does she mean recover from her leaving?"

"Mother started throwing things down the stairs," Abigail said. "The governess's things."

I could feel my face twist in disbelief. Why I doubted it even for a moment, I don't know. "Why would she do that?"

"Because…because the governess found out what Mother did today," Abigail said quietly. "But I'd rather not talk about it."

"Fine, Abigail, I won't press you, but I will speak to Mother if she did something to you," I said cautiously. I felt that any wrong word could result in not getting the information I wanted.

"That will only make it worse," Abigail said. Her voice was so very soft. "Father, is there nothing you can do to stop her from hurting me?"

It was physical. It had to be. I had to hide my face at that point. I covered it with my hand. Such sadness for someone just starting her life. I thought of sending her away then, to Europe, but she wouldn't know the first thing about taking care of herself. I couldn't send Christopher and Emma with her—they were still too young. This was my fault. It was all my fault. I never should have married Elizabeth, but how was I to know she would become this way?

As I lowered my hand from my face, I felt it shaking. It was rage. What is Elizabeth doing to me?

"I have tried, Abigail," I said, and I think my face must have been frightening because she took a step back. She should not fear her own parents. "But even…painful messages do nothing to dissuade her." I moved closer to her. "But you must remember something, Abigail."

She waited for me to speak again.

"The way she frightens you," I said. "If it frightens you, it would frighten her too. You must learn to help yourself sometimes."

God forgive me for the permission I gave today.

*

"Why didn't you tell me you'd given her a Bible?" Elizabeth hissed at Richard. She had cornered him in their bedroom while he was picking a suitable tie for later that evening. She was inches away from his face. "She told me it came from her former Sunday school teacher."

"She probably didn't want to make you angry," Richard said in a monotone voice, continuing his task and not looking up at her.

"I asked why *you* didn't tell me, Richard," Elizabeth said.

He turned around with the handkerchief in his hands. It was…

"Is that…" she whispered, unable to finish the sentence.

"In lieu of the dress you never had made," he said with no fluctuation in his voice. He tucked it down into his inner breast pocket, then pulled his jacket closed. He tapped it— right on his heart.

The handkerchief was the exact pattern of the wallpaper, the black and white damask that lined the whole upstairs. It was *exact*.

The man felt nothing. Nothing.

"Did you have that specially made?" Elizabeth asked, her voice raising and wavering unintentionally.

He didn't answer.

"Where?" she asked, more forcefully. "Who made that for you?" His silence was maddening. "Who!"

He smiled.

*

He'd worn it. That handkerchief. He'd worn it.

Elizabeth paced up and down their bedroom, a shared space of complete denial. Her nostrils flared for no one to see, and she could feel them move with every hateful thought. There was a looking-glass face down on the dresser. She stomped across the room and picked it up to see what she looked like—to see what he had made her.

It had to be the shadows in the room. The shadows cast by the oil lamp. It had to be.

Her brows angled down, slashes like those that could be made by nails in flesh. The wrinkles and creases that rippled up from them and into her forehead all the way up to her hairline were heavily outlined in darkness, only slim bits of skin still in light. At this angle, the arrow shape at the end of her nose was pronounced by the shadows, as if she had no nostrils at all. Her mouth…it seemed to be in a perpetual upside-down horseshoe, its light pink color an oddly feminine rupture through her hardened face, a shadow underneath to bring out a circle of chin. Her porcelain skin did not look breakable. Quite the opposite, it looked thick and impassable. She wondered when her dark eyes had developed their constant glint.

If only she hadn't married Richard.

If only she hadn't had that first child. That was where it had really begun.

She put the looking-glass down hard on the dresser. Too hard. She heard it shatter, a light but piercing tinkling sound of shards breaking and falling together. She picked up the looking-glass and found a long, jagged shard the length of the frame. Taking the shard between two fingers, Elizabeth gently picked it up and placed it in her other palm. It looked sharp, so very sharp all around. But the top tip was the most fascinating. It was like a mountaintop, a crescendo, and Elizabeth reached out to touch it with her index finger, just to see what it felt like. Her finger paused right above the point, mesmerized, before she raked it down across the whole pad of her finger and immediately took in a sharp breath between her clenched teeth. She shook her head as if waking up from a bad dream. The pain was searing, like nothing she had felt before. She was surprised by it, but she didn't regret it.

Everything was that child's fault.

She would wait until Abigail was away from her room the next day.

It would learn what it had done.

And she would learn something more about it.

October 15, 1856

Mother was late to breakfast, which was a very strange occurrence. She was never late, although sometimes she didn't come at all. She had been silent, her stern presence somehow overwhelming today, and Abigail's siblings didn't serve as buffers. Sometimes Abigail wondered whether they didn't even feel the tension Mother created. Perhaps it was only Abigail—and possibly Father—who felt it eating at their stomachs while they tried to eat their food.

Abigail had tried not to look at Mother too much, just focused on her meal, peeking nervously at her silent brother and sister, and asked to be excused immediately. She thought she'd felt Mother's eyes burning into her, but on the two occasions when Abigail had glanced up to check, Mother hadn't been looking at her at all. Sometimes Abigail wondered about her own sanity in this house.

While Christopher and Emma went into town, Abigail decided to take her Bible down to the willow tree that afternoon to disappear for a while. There had been some rain earlier, but she hadn't heard any since. There probably had not been enough to make it through the willow tree's thick strands of leaves. Abigail didn't bother to bring an umbrella. She didn't care for carrying one unless there was torrential downpour, and at that point it didn't do much anyway.

Walking to the willow, Abigail turned her face up toward the sky at the first tiny water droplet on her hand. The sun was brilliant, a pale shade of yellow that shone easily through the light gray clouds. Perhaps there would be a sun shower.

Abigail didn't bother to part the willow's long branches, she just walked right through them. A couple trailed over her shoulders and one brushed over her head. She liked the light feel of them. Today they were a little bit wet, of course. She didn't mind.

Under the willow tree it felt cooler and more stagnant than outside with no breeze able to blow through. It was safe.

She found her favorite sitting spot and leaned against the tree, staring at the thick wall of leaves in front of her. It was amazing how much something could grow in sixteen years. When Abigail was little, the tree's branches hadn't come anywhere near the ground, but now it was a full waterfall of greenery. The way she could see the light outside but not be touched by it was almost like a work of art. She wished she could paint.

Abigail put her finger where part of a dried willow branch lay in her Bible to keep her spot. It was the perfect way to mark her place. She slipped her finger between the pages and dragged it down inside the section.

"Ouch!" A sharp pain in her finger as it ran down something hard made her gasp; she pulled her finger out and held it up in front of her. Blood ran down her finger and onto her hand. The gash—and it was quite a gash—was pouring thick red blood. She felt her throat close a little with the pain. It was tempting to cry like a child, but she didn't. She held her hand out to the side so as not to get the blood on her dress or her Bible and opened the book with her other hand.

A long, jagged looking-glass shard was wedged in the pages with her dried willow, the willow broken in half from the force of the shard having been shoved inside. Blood ran along some of the shard's edge and stained the page of her book in a smear across the opposite page, where she'd inadvertently dragged her finger to get it out.

What on earth is a looking-glass shard doing in my Bible? Abigail frowned in thought, leaving her throbbing finger hanging, her arm still held out parallel with the ground and to her right. She had no idea where it had come from or why. She couldn't imagine who would do such a strange thing. The only cruel person in the house was Mother, of course, but still, why would she do that? It made no sense.

Thunder struck, breaking Abigail's train of thought, and she stood with her arm still held out and her finger dangling. She took her Bible and walked back to the house in a state of bewilderment.

October 16, 1856

When Abigail went to church Sunday morning along with everyone else, Elizabeth stayed home as usual. She stayed in bed and did not even bother to go downstairs and feign a headache. Although she was in bed, her eyes remained wide open, waiting.

Waiting.

She had to know.

Finally she heard the front door close and she jumped out of bed. Opening the door quietly, slowly, she peeked down the hall and listened. She could hear nothing at all. She tiptoed to Abigail's door and gently eased it open in case she happened to be there waiting for her. She peered around the room and saw nobody. Perfect.

From the doorway, Elizabeth looked carefully at every surface, trying to find the Bible without having to move things around. She didn't want to leave any sign she'd been there. It looked like the Bible wasn't sitting out, so Elizabeth would have to open some drawers. She found herself having a hard time stepping foot into Abigail's room; she felt as if something bad would happen if she did. She was afraid.

Elizabeth peered around again and noticed a lump under the bed covers. Could she have put it there? Nobody would bother to look in a bed for a book. It was actually quite a smart place to put something to hide it.

Perhaps not quite smart. Perhaps cunning, she corrected herself.

She approached the bed, leaned down, and pulled the sheets back. The Bible was indeed there. Tilting the top of the book toward her, she found a red stain that ran across a small section of pages.

It had worked. Abigail had learned what it meant to deceive Elizabeth.

Not even God could save her from that.

October 17, 1856

"Hello, Mr. Bartley."

"Miss Whitestone, hello," the pharmacist said. "May I help you find something?"

Abigail held out her hurt finger to show the pharmacist. "Can you tell me what I'd need to heal an injury like this?"

He frowned. "You know, Mrs. Whitestone was in here just yesterday looking for something to heal a cut a bit like that one. You could use the same ointment, if she still has it. She shouldn't have had to use much, like I told her." He laughed. "Funny, both of you coming in here for the same thing."

Abigail smiled, but her eyes remained hard. "Quite." She thought for a moment. "Was it also the looking-glass?" She enunciated every syllable sharply.

"Yes!" he said. "She broke her looking-glass. Like mother like daughter, it seems." He smiled wide.

"It does seem that way," she said. "Thank you."

*

After everyone was asleep, Elizabeth went downstairs to get the book she'd forgotten in the sitting room. She hoped she could read herself to sleep. She took an oil lamp with her to light the way, although she knew the house by heart. The lamp was just a precaution.

In the sitting room, Elizabeth spotted her book on the table and sat down on the couch for a moment, putting her lamp next to the book. She looked at the lamp on the wooden table and wondered… If she lit the table with the flame from the lamp, how long would it take to burn? To spread? How long would all that take? How long before everyone else smelled the smoke and ran downstairs? She toyed with the idea in her head. If the fire spread rapidly enough and the whole downstairs was ablaze before anyone realized, no one could come down to escape. And the second story window was too high to jump from. Perhaps one of them would try, but probably only one. Seeing that one jump and break something, seeing whoever it was land flat on the ground and too pained to yell up, would stop the others from jumping. They would all burn.

On the other hand, if the fire was too slow, they would all escape with no problem. The main question would always be why Elizabeth hadn't stopped the fire or called for help if the fire was her fault. She could most likely get away with saying Abigail did it. She could say she'd watched Abigail do it. No one would be any the wiser. But then again, Abigail would find Elizabeth after that no matter how far she ran, she knew it, and Abigail was capable of anything. Anything at all.

Elizabeth breathed in deeply, feeling her lungs expand her chest and wondering at how something that was supposed to be of her own flesh could be so terrifyingly evil. It was intrinsic. It was since birth. A mother should not fear her own daughter. It should only be the other way around.

Elizabeth sighed. Unless she could warn Emma and Christopher to get out, she would have bad memories of the whole thing anyway. Even just Emma…

Taking her book in her arms, she dismissed the whole idea. There were too many ways it could all go wrong. She picked up the lamp and walked slowly to the stairs, dread flushing through her at the thought of Richard lying there in bed, where she slept helplessly every night. She wished they had a big enough house for him to sleep elsewhere so she could lock her door against him and the other one while she rested. You could never tell what a wicked thing was capable of.

Elizabeth climbed the stairs slowly, putting her foot only on the front edge of each stair to avoid making too much noise. It was hard to keep quiet on wooden stairs, easier in the daylight than in the darkness so she could see the spots she knew made them squeak before she stepped on them.

When will they ever come up with a way to silence wooden st—

Elizabeth's foot slipped forward fast and she tumbled backward, falling to the landing hard on her back. The wind was forced out of her and she lay there, breathless and shocked. Her mind was completely blank for a few moments, trying to grasp the fact that she had fallen down the stairs. Not fallen, slipped. Slipped on stairs she'd just descended only a few minutes before.

The lamp.

She turned violently to find a patch of fire on the floor where the almost empty lamp had spilled oil that caught fire, and without thinking, she slapped her bare hands over it. It died with a few harsh pats. She righted the unbroken lamp immediately, although it was no longer lit.

With an oily, smarting palm gripping the lamp, she realized the pain in her upper back where she'd landed. She wouldn't clean the floor—Ashdon would notice and have it cleaned before they awoke.

And then she remembered why she'd fallen. A slippery spot.

Elizabeth dried her hands on her dressing gown and crawled over to the stairs carefully and slowly, not knowing what to expect. She couldn't see anything in the pitch black. She found the steps and put her hand on each one, feeling for whatever had caused her fall. On the fourth step, her fingers ran into something that pinched her skin hard She stuck her fingers in her mouth and tasted blood. Putting her hand above the stair, she slowly lowered it until she felt the coldness of something under her hand. She flattened her palm onto the object and tried to feel its shape. Jagged, cold, hard.

It couldn't be.

Without some light, she couldn't tell for sure. Carefully, she worked her hand around the object so she could hold it.

It was.

The looking-glass shard.

In the dark, Elizabeth's eyes widened until they stung to blink. She tried not to panic. There was only one person who possessed the shard. Had Abigail heard her come down and silently placed the shard on the stairs? Was it possible?

Elizabeth felt her breathing become ragged and tried to control her fears. She crawled the rest of the way up the stairs, even slower than before. She reached the landing at the top and crawled slower still. So slowly, she barely moved. One hand forward, opposite knee forward. Next hand forward, opposite knee forward. One hand—what was that? What was that under her hand? It felt like…like…

She squeezed the flesh of a foot and gasped, recoiling immediately. She heard a step. Another step. A door next to her creaking closed.

Elizabeth was frozen with fear, trembling in place.

"Goodnight, Mother," said Abigail's voice from behind the door.

October 18, 1856

Elizabeth stayed in bed all the next day. She didn't have to make an excuse to Richard; he never asked anymore when she stayed in bed. She listened to the steps around the house, listening closely in case any came too near to her door. Her heart skipped beats so often that her breathing became heavy and panicked.

What would she do if Abigail came into the room? What could she do?

Elizabeth twisted a lace handkerchief through her hands over and over, the constant feeling making her room feel smaller and smaller. Repetition in thought, repetition in action, repetition in fear. How long could this go on? She couldn't live like this forever.

Prayer? She had not visited church in so long…

There was only one verse that came to mind, only one thing she could repeat over and over again.

Repetition.

"The Lord is on my side; I will not fear: what can man do unto me? The Lord is on my side; I will not fear: what can man do unto me?"

She trembled harder. Last night had proven it: this verse was untenable.

20 years old
1860

May 14, 1860

Abigail walked the gardens in the park by herself. It wasn't proper for women to go walking alone. Normally a minimum of two women or a woman and a man would venture out together. But Abigail was never one for doing what was expected. What was expected was always whatever Mother wanted, and it was rare Abigail could allow herself to do as Mother told her. Most of the time Mother didn't speak to her, of course, but still, if Mother insisted, Abigail felt a catapult in her head, flinging the idea back out into the air. Usually Mother only wanted to humiliate Abigail or keep her out of sight anyway, just the way Mother had been out of sight for so long. She didn't really go out anymore.

The flowers were what fascinated Abigail. She loved how beautiful they were, how their flourishing brought not only lovely blooms, but scents that seemed almost heavenly. She could close her eyes and let the perfume of the flowers flow in and out of her for hours.

"Excuse me." A man's voice came from beside her.

Abigail startled, her whole body jumping embarrassingly. She put her hand over her heart.

"I'm so sorry, miss, I hope I didn't scare you," the man said, even though it was obvious that he had.

Abigail swallowed hard and then looked at him. She couldn't speak for a moment. She felt unprepared. Mother and Father had never taught her how to act around young men. Even at church, she'd never been introduced to anyone since she was a little girl, but especially not young men.

"It's just that," he continued, "I've seen you at Sunday services, but we've never been introduced. I know this is entirely improper, but no one is ever around to introduce us outside of church. And in it…well, a place of worship is hardly proper."

She watched his eyes go back and forth between her own. She still hadn't said a word.

"If someone were introducing us, I would be introduced as Mr. Scott," he continued. "Mr. Conrad Scott."

"Oh," was all Abigail could get out, breathily.

"You are Miss Abigail Whitestone, if I'm not mistaken?" He'd left out her middle name. Was that on purpose? Or didn't he know it? Perhaps she'd better not correct him. She preferred to be called Abigail anyway. It suited her best.

"Yes, sir," she said. She remained silent, her eyes sticking to his, trying to catch his eyes looking at something he disliked about her. A glance at her hair, a glimpse at her dress. But nothing. Just eye contact.

He laughed lightly. It was sweet, like he was calling her shy without actually saying it.

"Perhaps we could imagine our former Sunday school teacher introduced us so we have an alibi when our parents ask how we met?" He smiled conspiratorially at her, leaning in a little. His smile was like forgiveness for who she was always made to be.

"Yes, of course," she said gently, looking down at the flowers again.

"Do you like gardens, Miss Whitestone?" he asked patiently. "Or is it only the flowers themselves you admire?" He joined her in turning toward the flowers.

"I like everything about gardens," Abigail said after a pause. "I just think it's wonderful to watch something grow from nothing."

"I agree. Even though it can take quite some time for seeds to sprout and plants to come above ground, it's hard not to watch their progress every day. And it's worth the wait."

Abigail's gloved hands gripped each other so tightly, her knuckles were beginning to hurt.

"What's your favorite flower, Miss Whitestone?" Mr. Scott asked.

"Violets," she answered quickly, then immediately felt insecure about it. She should have said something more grand, more widely appreciated. More normal.

"Violets?" he asked, surprised, his voice higher. "I've never heard a lady say that before."

She felt like a fool.

"What makes you pick them over roses? Aren't roses what every lady wants from a gentleman?" he asked.

"You didn't ask what I wanted from a gentleman, you asked what I like," she said before she could stop herself. She felt brutal, but she also felt more like herself with an honest answer.

"For many ladies, those are one and the same," he said, "but not always for good reasons. Violets are common, but I agree that there is something fascinating about their vivid color and their ability to survive even when they look fragile."

Abigail was surprised Mr. Scott was having a real conversation with her, not just something superficial anymore. He had shared an opinion on "most ladies" and what he thought of them. She must have shocked him into speaking to her as if he knew her better, perhaps even as if she were a man. Did that mean a lack of respect? What did that mean? Anxiety twisted at her stomach. This was starting to feel like home. She didn't want the gardens to feel like home. That was the whole point of the gardens: to escape.

"It was very nice meeting you, Mr. Scott. I hope the rest of your day is pleasant," Abigail said quickly before walking away. She didn't wait for his reply.

*

As Abigail worked at her embroidery in the evening by the fire, her fingers moved mechanically. She'd never really spoken to a man socially before. It was nerve-racking. She had sorted out that her uncertainty and doubt of herself had made her anxiety rise so that it felt as if Mother had been staring at her while she spoke with Mr. Scott. Once she separated out that feeling, she realized another feeling. A floating feeling inside, as if all her organs were no longer held in place but were swimming about wherever they pleased. She was breathing harder too, even now.

Mr. Scott had been like nothing she'd ever seen before. Quite different from Father, and even young Christopher. Mr. Scott had fair skin, lightly freckled, smooth like porcelain. His smile overtook much of his face, accompanied by perfect teeth. His lips seemed to stretch forever to reveal a longer and longer line of teeth. Even though she'd barely been able to look anywhere but his eyes, she'd noticed his pronounced cheekbones that seemed to make straight down-slanted shadowed lines leading directly to his mouth. He was so unusual, beautiful and yet strange. Would all ladies think he was so attractive? She couldn't decide if he was attractive or just strangely engrossing; his face seemed like it could pull her in all of its own accord.

What a strange feeling.

But his face was all she could see.

May 15, 1860

Over the years, Abigail had learned to be afraid of hope, trying not to feel it, but it was an unavoidable emotion. No matter how much experience she gained with disappointment and pain, she kept on hoping. She hated it. Because the hope would mix with the fear of loss and disappointment as well as the anxiety of knowing and always being right about how things would end. Badly.

And yet Abigail found herself strolling the park gardens with a slight shakiness to her hands. She had gone to the park at exactly the same time as when she'd met Conrad, hoping—and hating herself for it—that she would bump into him again. How nice it would be to have a second chance to speak to him. She hadn't spoken much the first time, but perhaps this time she could be more conversational. Perhaps this time she could be more like a regular lady rather than the Whitestone she'd grown into. Then again, he'd seemed happy that she was different from the norm. So what should she do? She calculated and calculated as she looked at the flowers without seeing them. She'd thought about these same questions at home and still had come to no conclusion.

Well, realistically, how long could I pretend to be something I'm not before my facade starts to break down piece by piece? Strategy couldn't help her there. Eventually he would see her for herself. No, he had to want to spend time with her as she was. Otherwise there would be no assurance he would still want to speak to her if he met her family, which would surely happen in church. If she seemed like a slowly decaying sweetness, he would quickly become disillusioned and stop bothering with her. But if he really saw her awkward, well meaning, damaged self and still cared for her... She'd have him then. And she'd have him properly.

"Miss Whitestone, you look like you have a lot on your mind," said a voice next to her. She turned jerkily to see a gentleman she didn't know. That sinking feeling set in, the beginning of her disappearing hope. "Mr. Conrad said I might find you here."

Abigail swallowed hard and said, "Good afternoon," in a flat voice.

"My name is George Welton. You may have heard my last name before. Welton's Bakery?"

Abigail nodded and let a feeble smile form on her face. One that crumbled as soon as he began to speak again.

"I hope you don't find me rude, approaching you while you're alone, but Mr. Conrad said you might not mind." He paused, waiting for her approval.

"I don't," she said, intertwining her gloved hands in front of her.

"I'm glad to hear it. I won't bother you for long, just to give you this." Mr. Welton held out a book to her. "Mr. Conrad's mother has had another spell of illness, and he wanted to make sure you knew he hadn't forgotten you." Mr. Welton smiled. "I didn't ask any questions, Miss Whitestone, since Mr. Conrad is a private person. I just promised to deliver the message for him."

Abigail took hold of the book and slowly retracted her arm as if she hadn't decided whether to keep the book yet.

"Thank you," she said softly. Raising her eyes to his, she said more firmly, "If you see him, please tell him... please tell him I'll return it after I read it."

Mr. Welton shook his head. "It was intended as a gift,

Miss Whitestone."

"Oh," Abigail said, drawing out the word. She paused. Gifts were something she was unaccustomed to receiving. "Then please thank him for me."

"Of course," he said. "It was nice to meet you, Miss Whitestone. I hope to see you again soon." He took a step backward and tipped his hat.

"It was nice to make your acquaintance as well, Mr. Welton. Goodbye."

Abigail watched Mr. Welton walk away before she looked down at the book. It was beautiful—a black marbled hardcover with leather corners. When she turned it to read the leather spine of the book, she saw gold lettering identifying it as *The Black Tulip* by Alexandre Dumas. Upon opening it, a piece of stationery fell out. Abigail looked around as if afraid someone else could have seen this private shock. She placed the stationery back in the book and went straight home.

*

Abigail entered her house quietly, turning the doorknob slowly, but it caught constantly as it turned; it needed to be greased. She opened the door but saw and heard no one. Paying careful attention, she put the tip of her boot on the floor noiselessly and gently lowered the rest of her shoe down until the heel rested on the floor.

Mother hadn't known she'd gone out, and if Abigail got caught… It was impossible to predict the consequences. Never mind trying to cover up why she had a book in her hand that the family didn't own. Mother seemed to keep track of every little thing in the house so that if anything was out of place, missing, or new, she noticed immediately. Abigail could never understand how she kept a constant inventory like that.

By now Abigail had gotten her other foot in the door and was easing the heavy block of wood shut, turning the knob slowly again from the inside, then letting it go tiny bit by tiny bit until she could finally let go completely. It would take too long to remove her boots, what with their 20 buttonholes, so she'd have to be quite quiet walking across the foyer to the stairs. Patience was key. She stayed on the balls of her feet, careful not to touch her heels to the ground while she moved across the floor. Slowly, step by step, she made it to the stairs. She climbed them the same way she crossed the floor. When she reached the top step she took a short break. Mother was most likely in her room at the end of the hall. Abigail had to be totally silent on the short journey to her room. She was so close—

A movement. A movement from Mother's room. Abigail took a chance and quickly placed the book on the lower stair behind her before turning toward the hall again.

Mother opened the door.

Please don't go downstairs, please don't go downstairs...

Framed in the doorway, Mother stood completely still, the stiffness in her body showing in the muscles protruding from her neck. They stood facing each other, neither moving, for a few seemingly elongated seconds before Mother said, "Why are you standing there." It was a flat statement, but one that required a response.

"I was on my way to my room," Abigail said, and it wasn't a lie—she really was going there.

"Why are you standing there," Mother repeated dryly. Mother was an expert at communicating her deductions without actually saying them. And right now she was implying was that Abigail hadn't answered the question.

"I was being quiet so as not to wake you."

"I wasn't asleep," Mother said, speaking almost on top of Abigail's last word.

Abigail tried hard not to break eye contact. "Your door was closed, how was I to know—"

"You didn't know my door was closed when you came up the stairs," Mother said harshly. "And I didn't ask you why I didn't hear you, I asked why you are standing there." She waited. Mother's head tilted slightly. "How long have you been standing at the top of the stairs?"

Abigail didn't know what to say. She had no idea where the conversation was going, nor did she know what the correct answer would be, the answer that would make Mother stop.

"How long," Mother said flatly, no longer asking but demanding.

"Why don't you go to church?" Abigail asked. She didn't know exactly why she'd said it, but she did know it was equally impossible for Mother to answer that question as it was for Abigail to answer Mother's. If Abigail could just get to her room and close Mother out…

Mother frowned. "What?" she asked breathlessly and held her hand to her heart. "You wicked little thing."

"I am far from the only one who notices, Mother, that you only get headaches on Sunday mornings," Abigail said, gaining strength from Mother's obvious weakening. "I will answer your question if you will answer mine."

"What are you hiding?" Mother asked, taking a step forward. "You would never speak to me this way unless you were—"

"Careful, Mother," Abigail said, her quickening

heartbeat drowning out her own voice. "The stairs can be treacherous."

Mother visibly shrank back into herself, and Abigail felt, mixed in with her fear, a growing central heat of control.

"Go back to your room," Abigail said, stepping forward.

Mother hesitated, and Abigail decided to take a chance and walk past her. She walked quickly but rigidly, with no slouch or wince as she passed even though she was deathly afraid. She went into her room and closed the door behind her, immediately putting her ear up against it to listen for Mother's footsteps. Abigail had left the book on the stairs. This time Mother could hurt herself without Abigail intending it.

She listened as Mother walked toward the stairs, and she clenched her skirts in both hands, her stomach tight, uncertainty keeping her from making a move to stop Mother. What if she did run out and tell Mother not to go downstairs? She would have to explain why. And if she explained there was something on the stairs she could slip on…

Quick footsteps walked back past her door as Mother went back to her room and slammed the door. Abigail's heart didn't stop pounding, but her head cleared of everything until all she felt was relief. She eased her door open and peeked down the hall at Mother's room. No one. Should she be quick or quiet? She couldn't be both in her shoes, and it would take too long to unbutton them. She exhaled heavily. All this figuring all the time, all this guessing and scheming. Sometimes she just felt so tired of it all. It was so extreme, so unbelievable. If she sent this story in to a magazine, they would send it back and say it was unrealistic.

But it wasn't. Not for Abigail.

She slid her bedroom slippers tightly over her shoes to stifle the sound the heel would inevitably make. Then she snuck to the stairs slowly and kneeled to pick up the book. She heard nothing from behind her. She snatched it to her chest and went back to her room, shutting the door quickly and without a sound.

Finally.

Abigail went to her writing desk and held the book by the spine so the letter would fall out. She laid *The Black Tulip* down and sat with the letter in her hands. It was short, but since she'd never received a letter before, it was so exciting that she read the words out of order at first, then had to start again.

Dear Miss Whitestone,

I regret that I could not meet you in the gardens today. I already remember yesterday with great fondness. As my mother is ill, I feel I must stay by her side until she is better. However, her bouts of illness are usually quite short lived. I will write as soon as I am able to leave the house again. I hope you will honor me with another meeting, perhaps this time with your parents. I would very much like to meet them. Of course I will understand if you do not accept my company, but I certainly hope you do.

Sincerely,

Conrad Scott

His address was not included, so she could not respond. She assumed he had done that on purpose. Perhaps a man like Mr. Scott was used to acceptance, or perhaps he had forgotten to include it.

Abigail could not stop her heart from jumping with both joy and anxiety. Asking to meet her parents was a very good thing, but... She couldn't introduce Mother, and Mother would never agree anyway. It would have to be Father. But she had never asked for such a thing. How should she go about it?

Lost and unwilling to ask Emma for help—she couldn't stand someone else knowing of her pain if he never wrote again—Abigail walked to the bed and placed the letter under her pillow. At least for tonight she could dream of happiness. At least until his next letter came.

May 19, 1860

A few days later, when Abigail came downstairs for breakfast, she saw a beautiful bouquet of flowers in a cut glass vase in the middle of the dining room table. The vase had been Abigail's grandmother's, something Mother kept hidden away and never ever used. Nobody knew why Mother was so unwilling to use it, but the Whitestones kept away from it no matter what.

The central flowers were a vibrant red, some with bright yellow at the base of their petals. Surrounding them were smaller multi-layered flowers, some of white, some of cornflower blue, and some of pink.

Abigail took a step toward them, captivated by their loveliness. There were never flowers in this house. They seemed like the only living things she'd even seen here, beautifully out of place. So alive.

"They came for *you*," Emma said softly from behind Abigail. "The man brought a card and said they were for you." Abigail turned around and Emma held the little card out for her. Abigail took it gingerly, slowly, as if it might disappear at any moment.

Red kennedia for your intellect, love in a mist for my curiosity.

She turned the card over and found more writing on the back.

I would be a lucky man if you would meet me in the park again.

Abigail looked up at Emma and couldn't help the enormous smile that crossed her face. "Here, read it!" she said, putting aside her usual resentment masked as neutrality toward Emma. Normally they stayed out of each other's way, although Emma had never seemed to dislike Abigail. Rather she typically seemed a bit intimidated. Abigail didn't understand why; if anything, she should be intimidated by Emma's beauty and good social graces, especially now that Emma was sixteen. In becoming a woman, now Emma was competition on top of it all. Nevertheless Emma's clear unease underscored their every interaction, as did Abigail's coldness. Naturally this kind of male attention overrode their routine awkwardness.

Emma grabbed the card from her and read it front to back.

She gasped and looked up with a matching smile. "Do you know who it's from?"

"It's from a man named Mr. Scott. I met him in the park earlier this week. We were introduced. Apparently he attends our church, but I've never seen him before. I've never received flowers from a man!"

"Are you going to meet him in the park?" Emma asked.

"I will. I definitely will," Abigail said, sounding breathless. "Oh Emma, you'll have to help me make sure my hair is just right. I didn't look like anything special when I met him, but I should make sure I look better this time." Abigail's heart beat so fast it was almost painful. Her eyes couldn't focus on anything for more than a second. She had never felt like this before, so…appreciated. Being the object of someone's interest was both exciting and daunting. She hadn't even tried to impress him last time. What if she did try this time and he didn't like her anymore? What had she done right? How could she duplicate it?

"What is that." It wasn't a question. Mother stood behind Emma as if appearing out of nowhere. Her usual *clunk clunk* hadn't been heard.

"They're flowers, Mother!" Emma exclaimed. She seemed just as excited as Abigail. "They're for Abigail."

"Abigail?" Mother said the name slowly, sounding out each syllable in a creaky voice that rose from her lowest octave.

Abigail nodded harshly. She had no idea what to say. She didn't want Mother to ruin this for her, neither this moment nor this new feeling.

"Yes, Mother. They're from a man who seems to admire me." She was businesslike in her tone, and she stepped forward briskly and thrust the card out at Mother, practically right into her hands.

Mother read the whole card.

"A man…" she mumbled. "What man."

"A man I was introduced to in the park by a mutual acquaintance."

"What mutual—"

"He attends our church. His name is Mr. Scott. You can ask whomever you'd like." Abigail couldn't make the excuse of the Sunday school teacher introducing them as Mr. Scott had planned. That lie hadn't gone well with the Bible, and it had proven that Mother would check on anything Abigail said. She had to be careful, steer her away from naming a name.

As Mother's mouth opened in a sneer to say something more, Abigail thought fast of what might stop her. "Since you never attend, you'll want to ask someone." Mother's mouth closed. "I'm sure Mrs. Hinsley would know him. She knows everyone. So check with her."

Mother grimaced visibly.

This was the chance to escape without further

explanation. She breezed quickly by Mother as she said, "I'll be upstairs and Father can take me to the park later to meet Mr. Scott."

"Your father won't take you," Mother yelled, a severe edge to her voice. It sounded like it could cut.

Abigail paused at the bottom of the steps without turning around. "Then Mrs. Hinsley will take me." And with that, she fled to her room and shut the door.

*

Mother seemed to disappear after Abigail had gotten away with her evasive tactics. She had thought Mother would be waiting for her downstairs or even in the hallway that afternoon, but she wasn't. Abigail didn't search for her.

Mrs. Hinsley was only a few houses away from theirs, and after Emma helped make sure Abigail's hair was secured in place, Abigail went to see Mrs. Hinsley. She would understand. And she would help her. Abigail had put the pearl- and gold-framed eye pin on her underskirts for good luck. She didn't want to put it on the neck of her shirt in case Mr. Scott interpreted that as another man pursuing her. She had to be very careful how she handled this.

Abigail knocked on Mrs. Hinsley's door and waited. She wasn't on the stoop for long before the butler answered.

"Abigail Whitestone calling for Mrs. Hinsley," Abigail stated.

The butler opened the door wider and said, "Please come in, Miss Whitestone. Mrs. Hinsley is in the sitting room. Please wait while I tell her you're here."

"I'll show myself in, thank you." Abigail walked past the butler.

"Miss Whitestone, please, she already has a guest," the

butler said urgently, rushing after her.

"Mrs. Hinsley and I have an understanding," Abigail said arrogantly, opening the door and walking into the room. Mrs. Hinsley sat in the chair farthest from the door and Father sat in the chair closest to hers, separated by a small round table with a tea set on it. "Oh...Father. What are you doing here?" she asked.

Father sat up. Were his cheeks turning pink? He smiled a small half-circle. Abigail had never seen Father flustered before. Come to think of it, she had never seen him outside their own house before. Never except for at church.

"Your mother couldn't come to visit Mrs. Hinsley, so I came alone, Abigail. Don't mention this to her, it will just upset her. She wasn't happy to miss this engagement."

Abigail's eyes traveled from Father's to Mrs. Hinsley's, who didn't seem disturbed. She asked, "Where is Mr. Hinsley?"

"Called away, dear," she said easily and motioned toward a chair across the room. "Business. Collins, will you move that chair over here for Miss Whitestone?"

The butler moved with extraordinary quickness of foot and left immediately afterwards.

Abigail walked to the chair and sat down slowly. She put up a thin smile. *How odd.*

"How nice to see you during the week, Abigail. Are you well?" Mrs. Hinsley asked, sipping her tea nonchalantly.

"Y-yes, thank you, Mrs. Hinsley. And how are you?"

"Quite well, my dear."

The butler reappeared with an extra teacup and saucer for Abigail. He turned his back to Mrs. Hinsley, pushed the cup into Abigail's hands, and widened his eyes at her quite distinctly before getting the teapot off the table and filling

Abigail's cup. Then he left again, closing the door with finality.

"You look particularly well today, Abigail," Mrs. Hinsley commented, looking at Abigail's hair. "Something's different about you."

"Thank you. I did come to talk with you about something very delicate. In fact I wanted to ask you a favor. I..." Abigail didn't know how to start, especially with Father there. Mother was probably right that Father wouldn't take her to meet Mr. Scott, so she hadn't planned on his knowing except through Mother's complaints. But perhaps this was best. Perhaps this time she could tell her side of the story without Mother's twisting things and interfering.

"You see," Abigail started again, "I received some flowers today."

"Flowers! From whom?" Mrs. Hinsley cut into Abigail's last word, leaning forward in her chair. Abigail caught her father's sidelong look, the curling of his mouth on one side.

"They're from a Mr. Scott. We were introduced in the park a few days ago," Abigail said carefully. She had to say it exactly in the right way so that it sounded the same to everyone who heard the story. If Mother found out about any difference...

"Go on," Mrs. Hinsley said at Abigail's pause. "Is it Mr. Conrad Scott who attends our church?"

Our. It sounded like...family.

"Yes," Abigail said, starting to warm to the whole situation. This was quickly becoming comfortable. "He's so very nice, Mrs. Hinsley, he talked to me about the beautiful flowers in the gardens in town and was very polite."

"What did he send you?" Mrs. Hinsley asked, her eyes sparkling.

Abigail moved forward to sit on the edge of her seat. She felt so animated, so alive. It was a feeling unlike anything she'd felt before. "His note said kennedia and love in a mist, and he said they meant—"

"You don't have to tell me what they mean, my dear, I'm very well studied in the language of flowers," Mrs. Hinsley said. "*Those* are a *very* good sign." She nodded to confirm her confidence in her statement.

"He asked to see me again today in the gardens," Abigail said softly, unsure of the reaction she might get from each of them. She looked back and forth between them while they looked at each other. Mrs. Hinsley seemed to read a question in Father's face, one Abigail herself couldn't see.

"Mr. Scott is a very good man from an excellent family," Mrs. Hinsley said. "His father is inherently wealthy in ways I can't possibly fathom. A very good family indeed." To Father, "He would be an excellent match for our Abigail."

Our Abigail? That was awfully intimate. But perhaps she just said it because she was fond of Abigail. After all, Mrs. Hinsley had known Abigail since she was born. Still, what a strange thing to say. And yet…Abigail found that she didn't really mind, she was simply taken aback.

"I remember meeting his father a few times before," Father said, looking off. "He was a good conversationalist indeed."

They both turned back to Abigail.

"Well?" Mrs. Hinsley said. "Mr. Conrad is certainly interested in deepening your acquaintance. Will you accept him?"

Abigail paused. "I'd certainly like to," she said, a hesitation in her voice. She looked to Father.

He looked into her eyes for a moment before he said, "I approve." Abigail's heart felt as if it could break through her ribcage.

"Will you accompany me to meet him?" Abigail asked excitedly, breathlessly. She hoped Mother had been wrong that Father wouldn't come.

"I will, Abigail," he said, and smiled fully. Mrs. Hinsley smiled too.

*

As Abigail and her father approached the park, her hands fidgeted with her skirts. Father reached over and touched her elbow gently. She jumped at the contact. Nobody but Emma ever touched her.

"It will be fine," Father said, looking her in the eye.

Abigail wanted to tell him that Mother hadn't thought he'd come, and how thankful she was that he was there. This was the closest they'd been in a long time, physically and emotionally. But she didn't want to ruin the mood by bringing up Mother. So she nodded in what came out more like a neck spasm and looked for Mr. Scott.

Father pointed at some bright pink flowers in a pattern with white ones. "Those are lovely," he said, stopping in front of them.

"Yes, they are," Abigail said, her breath quickening. "I often think they're blushing with some secret, and the white ones don't know it." She laughed lightly. Father turned and walked toward another patch of flowers.

"Miss Whitestone?" Abigail heard from a short distance. She looked in the direction of the voice and saw

Mr. Scott already taking off his hat to greet her.

"Hello, Mr. Scott," she said more confidently than expected. She couldn't stop her lips from forming an open smile. He smiled back, and the brilliance of his teeth made her weak with happiness. *He is so beautiful.*

"Mr. Scott," Father said authoritatively, holding out his hand.

"Mr. Whitestone, I'm glad to see you," Mr. Scott said. He took the hand confidently and they shook once before letting go. "How are you today, sir?"

"Very well, thank you. I hear you have sent my daughter flowers," Father said. Abigail wasn't sure where this was going. Father only knew about them from Abigail's conversation—he hadn't actually seen them.

"Yes, sir. I hope I have your approval to deepen my acquaintance with Miss Whitestone." He seemed to know exactly what to say. He was so well bred.

Father smiled. "You have more than my approval, Mr. Scott. You have my invitation to visit my home."

What? Abigail thought that was faster than expected. But what did she know about these things? Mother never taught her.

"Thank you, sir," Mr. Scott said, his eyebrows raised. "I will certainly come by…tomorrow?"

"It would be my pleasure to have you," Father said.

"Thank you. I'm very much looking forward to it." Mr. Scott turned to Abigail and smiled a smile that seemed special and private. "I'm happy you liked the flowers."

Abigail could only smile back. She felt as if she would cry.

"Goodbye, Mr. Scott. Until tomorrow," Father said, taking a step back. Abigail stepped with him, following his lead.

"Goodbye, Mr. Whitestone, Miss Whitestone." He took off his hat, pressed his lips together and nodded. The edges of his lips still maintained their curve toward his ocean-blue eyes. An ocean she could escape on.

May 20, 1860

The time that Conrad would visit hadn't been set, but he'd asked to call today, so Abigail assumed he would keep his word. She woke early and paced in her room before coming down to breakfast. A man had never paid a visit to the house for her before. She wondered if she would be expected to sit with Father and Conrad or whether they wanted to be alone. She fretted over what to wear; no matter what, Conrad would surely see her and talk to her, if just for a few minutes.

She finally decided on a deep blue dress with a back peplum and high white collar. At the base of the neck of the dress, she wore her baptism pin with the brilliant blue eye so much like her own. The little pearls lining the eye-like shape of the piece were a nice touch but not too much for a day at home. It was the only jewelry she had.

Just before four o'clock in the afternoon, there was a knock at the door. Abigail stood in the parlor and heard the maid invite Mr. Scott inside. She walked out to meet him in the hall.

"Hello, Mr. Scott," she said. "How nice to see you."

Conrad took off his hat and handed it to the maid. "Good afternoon, Miss Whitestone," he said with his wide smile. "I hope you're feeling well today."

"I am, thank you," she said. After just slightly too long of a pause, she stumbled to ask, "A-and you?"

"Quite well now," he said.

"Ashdon, please tell Father Mr. Scott is here," Abigail said. She was doing better than she thought she would so far. "We'll be in the parlor for now."

"Yes, miss," the maid said and went off to deliver the

message.

"Please come in," she said, walking into the parlor.

"Thank you." He followed her and when she sat down on the couch, he sat in the armchair opposite. "You have a beautiful home in a very nice area of town."

"It's very convenient," Abigail said. She was already lost for words. She was terrible with filling gaps in conversation because she had no practice. Their family meals were fraught with tension and the less talking there was the better. She had never learned properly.

"Have you been enjoying the book I sent you?" Conrad asked.

"Oh yes," Abigail said, "it's very nice to read something so recently published. I haven't read anything modern."

"Oh? What do you usually read?"

"Mostly the Bible my father gave me," Abigail answered honestly. "I'm afraid you won't find me well informed."

"That's all right," Conrad said. "I could inform you in my letters."

She liked his implication of a future to their relationship, however small it was.

"I would like that."

"There's only one thing I must know before Mr. Whitestone comes in," Conrad said, frowning and leaning forward. "I hope I don't upset you, but your pin appears to be a mourning pin."

Abigail was taken aback. She hadn't thought of it that way before. "No, it's not."

"Then why are you wearing an eye brooch with a frame of pearls?" he asked.

"Oh no, this was a baptism present," Abigail said. "I've had it all my life."

His frown didn't disappear. "An unusual present for a baby," he said.

"I've asked both of my parents who gave it to me many times, but neither can seem to remember," she said. "I always like to think of it as someone I don't even know watching over me."

"That's a nice way to think of it," he said. He didn't seem satisfied.

"Ah, Mr. Scott," Father said, coming into the room. "Good to see you." He held out his hand.

Conrad stood and shook it. "Thank you for the invitation, Mr. Whitestone. I hope I haven't come at an inconvenient time."

"Certainly not, I'm just about to have tea. Will you join me?" Father asked.

"It would be my pleasure. Thank you."

"Abigail, we'll be in the sitting room if you need me," Father said, and Abigail was grateful for his subtle instructions for her not to join them.

*

As soon as Richard and Conrad entered the sitting room, Richard tugged the bell pull by the fireplace. The maid came immediately.

"We will take tea in here, Ashdon," he said, then sat down. Conrad took the seat across from him.

"Your home is very attractive," he said.

"Thank you," Richard said, "it's comfortable."

"I couldn't help but notice the wallpaper you have by the stairs. It's quite striking."

"That it is, but I hope you never have it in your own

home."

"Why is that?" Conrad asked.

"It takes quite a bit of work to keep up, and not everyone will like it."

"I'm not sure I would be brave enough to commit to something like that," Conrad said. "If I changed the walls in my home, they would remain solid colors. I hope you don't think me a coward."

"I think you're logical," Richard said. "There are times I wish I'd never gotten that wallpaper. Then there are other times I feel quite justified."

September 12, 1860

Abigail brought her embroidery down from her room and sat with it in her favorite armchair in the sitting room. Father was the only other person in the room, reading a newspaper. He seemed fidgety, tapping his finger on the back of the paper as he read.

"Oh, Abigail," Father said suddenly, looking up from his reading, "Mr. Scott will visit later for tea. I saw him today and asked him to come. He will be visiting with me alone."

Father had been encouraging every opportunity to chaperone Abigail and Conrad, and this was the first mention since May of a meeting without Abigail. Her heart fluttered, but she couldn't make assumptions. She was surprised Mother hadn't interfered yet. Father must have had some influence over her that stopped her from doing so. Fortunately Father had told Conrad very early on that Mother wasn't well and did not see visitors often. Conrad had not asked any questions, and for the first time, Mother's absence from church was a good thing. It fit into Father's excuse perfectly.

"Thank you, Father, for your willingness to get to know Mr. Scott," Abigail said, smiling at him. She was surprised at his efforts but was not about to second-guess them. Rather she wanted to encourage them as much as possible.

"It's important," Father said. "You need him."

"Need him?" Abigail asked. She knew that she "needed" him if she were to escape Mother. Was that what he meant? Did he really recognize that?

His eyes stayed on her, but his head lowered. He spoke low. "You need to leave."

Abigail felt immediate panic at Father's words, her heartbeat running away from her. So he did know her misery and hadn't said anything all these years. And now… what had happened to make him say this? The shadows in the room seemed to darken and deepen before her.

"What do you mean?" she asked, staring into his eyes. They seemed intent on getting his point across.

He sat back and, for the first time in front of her, looked sad. "You can't see it happening, can you?" he asked. His eyes moved jerkily around her face, examining. He tilted his head, tightened his lips into a straight line, and sighed heavily.

She knew what he was thinking. Did he really think she was truly like Mother? Didn't he know that she only behaved like Mother when she was defending herself on those frequent occasions when Mother was cruel toward her? She never acted like that toward anyone other than Mother—she thought. Had she started acting that way all the time? Had it seeped into her actual self? She realized her hands were gripping the arms of the chair so tightly that her fingertips were starting to hurt.

"There it is," he said.

Before Abigail could jump out of her seat and…and what, she didn't know, Father continued, "We need to get you out of here. You're still Abigail and I don't want to see that disappear completely. There's still time. There's still Mr. Scott."

Abigail couldn't decide whether to be thankful or angry; thankful that he saw her true self and wanted to save it, or angry that he wanted to give her off to another man to fix her issues instead of helping her himself.

Even in her mind, she paused. *Which feeling is more*

like Mother? Her lips quivered as she realized that she didn't know. The distinction was disappearing. Father was right. She needed to get out.

September 13, 1860

Abigail quietly eased the door closed after Conrad escorted her home, and she silently tiptoed to the stairs. She'd never gotten home this late before. In fact, she hadn't gone out at night before. She'd never been to parties and the opera; everything was new to her.

She got halfway up the stairs before her heart flew into her throat at the sight of half a woman's figure at the top of the stairs.

It was Mother.

Abigail could only see Mother's silhouette from the waist down; her waist to her head was coated in darkness. A dim oil lamp sat on the candle stand down the hall.

"That boy isn't to come here again, Abigail Delilah," Mother said in a deep, low voice. Her tongue seemed to curl around "Delilah" in a way that warped the "l" sound, and it disgusted Abigail. Her face crunched at the pronunciation and she wished she could somehow wipe it off her. But there was nowhere to wipe it off. It was her name. The name Mother had given her. And it was just the filthy way it was pronounced. There was no matter to it, no form it took or part of her it plastered itself onto, and yet she felt the intense urge to wipe off her cheek, her arm, and anything else she could until the feeling went away. But she didn't move.

"He will come here when he wants to, Mother," Abigail said, her voice just as low and deep. Her own voice surprised her; it mimicked Mother's too closely. Immediately her mind tried to alter the sentence she'd just heard herself speak. *My voice was softer than hers, it wasn't as harsh. There was no edge to my voice.* But some part of Abigail knew these replacements of the truth were just that.

Mother didn't move. She stood completely still and Abigail still could only see her from the waist down, just the skirt of her robe.

"You will not continue to see him," Mother said in the same voice as before. Her lack of upset at Abigail's blatant contradiction made her burn with frustration and anger. She wasn't being taken seriously. She was *never* taken seriously.

Mother turned around and took a step to walk away. Abigail climbed another step.

"I will, Mother," she said. "I will see him whenever I want to." She climbed another step. Only three more stairs to go before Abigail was on the landing and could get to her room and safely tuck herself away in bed. But she had to get past Mother first. A fear she loathed within herself stopped her from continuing up the steps. The frustration inside her burned hotter.

It looked like Mother was twisting around to look at Abigail, but the darkness kept her from seeing if that was the case.

"I already disposed of the flowers," Mother said as if something as simple as that ended a courtship. Her voice was cold and stern, not an emotion to be heard. Just fact. Just the knowledge that she would win, that she would get her way as always.

Abigail's head began to buzz and her eyes had a hard time concentrating on what she could see of Mother's robe. Mother had taken living things that represented love for Abigail and made them trash, *made them garbage*. They had been beautiful and they had meant so many things to

Abigail. So many things that Mother was taking away from her.

Abigail lifted a trembling leg and climbed another step and then another. Only one more left, but her legs were frozen again.

"Throwing away my flowers only means something to you," Abigail said, her voice shaking. She hated that her voice was shaking. She hated that Mother knew she was winning. Like always. "Nothing has changed between Mr. Scott and me." Her teeth began to chatter clearly and loudly before Abigail closed her lips to stifle the sound. Her jaw clenched tighter…tighter… It felt like it could never open again.

"I threw away your Bible, too," Mother said. Abigail couldn't tell which way Mother was facing anymore, she'd lost track of whether or not the robe had turned around. Then, very slowly and perfectly enunciated, Mother said, "I don't know how you ever read it without burning up alive."

Another step and Abigail was on the landing. Her hands grabbed at Mother's robe, clutching fistfuls of cloth and skin. Mother's back was to her, she could feel that now. Mother gasped; Abigail didn't even try to cover her mouth. Abigail gripped skin and cloth tighter, digging her fingers and knuckles into flesh and fabric as hard as she could. She whipped Mother around, spinning them both in a half-circle. She was in control of Mother—the only control necessary. For the first time, Abigail was in control even though she didn't completely know what she was doing.

She pulled Mother close, not loosening her grip, and growled in a voice foreign to her, "My tears have been my meat day and night, while they continually say unto me, Where is thy God?" She shook Mother back and forth, then held her still again and growled into her ear, "He is here now, finally." Abigail shoved her fists forward so forcefully that her arms flew out straight and she nearly fell to the floor. Hard thuds and blunted bangs thundered down the stairs as she realized Mother was tumbling down. She stood at the top and stared directly ahead into the dark with wide gaping eyes, hands at her sides, as she heard the final thump of Mother's body hitting the ground floor. Finally, mercifully, Mother was silent. The malice that always hung in the air like jaws about to bite was gone.

*

Abigail hadn't quite registered in her head what had just happened even though she'd done it herself. Her whole body began to tingle and quake all the way through. She didn't know what to do with herself. She couldn't think; her mind was blank and wouldn't wake up out of its state of shock.

Her eyes registered a light coming from behind her, but she couldn't move. She felt her throat close in a spasm of attempted tears that wouldn't come.

"Abigail?" Father's voice whispered.

Abigail could not turn around.

"Abigail, what was all that noise?" Father insisted, still whispering.

Abigail remained still but sucked in a shallow, noisy breath. Finally she could feel her limbs as parts of her that could move again. She tipped herself to the right and leaned against the wallpaper, quaking even more violently. Her head turned so slowly she wasn't sure if she was moving at all. Father quickly descended the stairs with his oil lamp, and she heard him gasp. When he reached the second floor landing again, his free hand found Abigail's shoulder. The single thing she could think was that this was only the third time she'd felt her father's touch: when he had given her the Bible, when he met Conrad, and now, when she'd killed Mother. She felt an overwhelming sense of dependency, and tears finally flooded her eyes so that she couldn't see. She felt her face melt into some horrific form of open terror that she couldn't even imagine. A high-pitched sound was emitting from her throat and she couldn't control it. Her lungs were losing all their air to that strange noise. Her knees buckled beneath her and she sank to the ground and gasped a breath so sudden and violent and large into her already swollen throat that it emitted a stuttering sound. She coughed hard and looked up at her father.

Emma poked her head out of her doorway. "What's going on?" she whispered. Father quickly turned around and took large steps to get to Emma, keeping his lamp light in her eyes so she couldn't get a good view of Abigail.

"Mother had an accident," he said quickly.

"What?" Emma said with immediate concern. "What ha—"

"She doesn't want you to come outside. She's em-embarrassed," Father stammered. "She'll be fine, I'm sure of it. Just go back to bed and I'll tell you about it tomorrow." This amount of talking and explanation was unusual for Father, but Emma's mixture of sleepy and stunned left her confused, and she didn't seem to realize how little sense any of this made.

"You don't need help?" Emma asked, rubbing an eye.

"No, no, just get back to sleep," Father said, shaking his head for emphasis.

Father stood there until Emma slowly closed the door

and he heard the latch click into place. Then he stood in front of Christopher's door and listened intently for any movement. Nothing. Christopher was a heavy sleeper, but Father stood there for quite some time before he was satisfied and came back to Abigail's side. He crouched in front of her.

"What happened here, Abigail?" he whispered quietly but with force. He gripped her shoulder and looked into her eyes steadily. Abigail shook her head. "Tell me, Abigail. Just tell me the truth. What happened?" Something in his eyes that she couldn't define made her believe wholeheartedly that she could trust him.

"She was taking everything from me, everything I had." Abigail tried to whisper, but some squeaks of her voice still escaped.

"What do you mean?" Father asked patiently.

"She told me I couldn't see Conrad anymore and she threw away the flowers he sent me and she threw away my Bible and she told me the Bible should've burned me. She always thought I was some kind of devil, why—" Father put his finger over Abigail's still trembling lips. She was getting too loud. She lowered his hand with her own. "I've only ever had this one happiness, this is all I've ever had, it's all I've had my whole life," she said, searching his eyes for pity. He looked down and nodded silently. He sniffed.

"I know. I know," he said, barely audible. After a few moments he looked back up at her. His eyes were red. His lips twitched before he said, "We will take care of this, Abigail."

She was overwhelmed—too many thoughts and questions wanted to come out of her mouth at once, but he took her hand warmly with his.

"Listen to me," he said. "We will make things right. She fell down the stairs in the dark at night."

Abigail nodded profusely and thought fast, thoroughly running over this idea in her head. But wait. She had grabbed Mother. What if she'd left marks on her skin? Abigail couldn't remember if she'd felt skin when she'd grabbed Mother's robe. It was all an uncertain blur of fear and outrage. She wasn't sure if she regretted it.

Father saw that Abigail was working something out without him. "What, Abigail, tell me."

"I-I may have left marks on her back. I grabbed her, but I don't remember if I grabbed her skin. If there's a bruise…"

Father thought for quite some time without moving anything but his eyes. Finally he gripped her hand tighter and urged, "Say it was me."

"What good will that do?" Abigail asked. Why would he say that?

He paused for a moment. "Abigail, everyone knows of the poor relationship between Elizabeth and me. It would be…for lack of a better term, acceptable to them for it to have been my doing."

"It would be the same for me," Abigail said. "They all know Mother despises me."

Father did not deny it. Instead he said, "You are young and have an opportunity for happiness with Conrad. You cannot be accused of murder when your life is finally coming around."

So her misery had truly always been plain to everyone. Abigail was overwhelmed with embarrassment, sadness for her life, for herself at being considered a piteous girl with a piteous existence. And that no one had bothered to help her, to make it better…had she really been so helpless all along? So pathetic? Was the only way to take control of her life now in the most deplorable manner? Was there any other way? It was all so confusing and overwhelming. She could feel no worry or distress, only self-pity intensified by a lifetime of pity from others.

Father must have noticed her will weakening because he said, "Abigail, you must let me do this for you."

She stared at him solemnly. "But I don't want you to leave me," she said honestly. Having him now was better than never having him at all.

"I have to leave to avoid arrest. I will leave tonight and you will send for the police at once. Say you saw me push her and that you couldn't stop me from leaving." He paused. "And you must wake Christopher and Emma after I've left and tell them the same story. I'll leave a note, too." At Abigail's wide eyes he said, "I will write to you as soon as I'm safe, in a day or two, and we can write always."

Abigail swallowed. "You'll write? Please promise. I can't bear to think of not hearing from you. I wouldn't have what little joy I have if it weren't for you, Father."

He smiled slightly. "I will write, Abigail. In one or two days. I promise."

September 14, 1860

Emma woke up far earlier than usual the following morning. She couldn't sleep any later because of all the nightmares darkening her mind, causing her to wake up frequently. Nightmare after nightmare of the wallpaper in the hallway, vague voices she couldn't understand drifting down the hallway. In the dream, Abigail's face was completely normal, staring, unblinking. Emma had a vague recollection of careful tears falling down one of Abigail's cheeks in the dream, but it was only a shimmer of a stream. Abigail had stared back at Emma with no change to her face. All Emma knew in the dream was that everything was frightening, everything. Nothing was moving, Abigail remained where she was, causing no immediate threat, and yet her dream throbbed with fear, her heart beating so loud and fast that it woke her up over and over again, sweat covering her forehead.

Father did not appear in the dream. Just Abigail, sitting in the hallway, her face vivid against the wallpaper. And that pounding feeling of extreme fear.

Emma couldn't help but get up just as the sun was starting to rise. She sat up in bed, making a conscious effort not to make any noise in doing so. Her breathing was silent, slow. If someone else had been in the room, they would never have known Emma was breathing at all. She sat frozen upright, unsure what to do with herself. She still felt afraid.

Thinking of the night before, the strangeness of it all started to come forward in her head. Mother had...she'd had a fall but was embarrassed. And Father had told Emma to go back to bed. Emma had caught a glimpse of Abigail but nothing of Mother before Father's frame had intentionally filled her vision. She had been too sleepy and confused to oppose him, and she'd felt herself instinctively drawing back into her room for reasons she still didn't grasp. Why hadn't she asked more questions? Why hadn't she just gone out into the hall to help? And why hadn't she seen Mother? Where had Mother's accident happened? Obviously not in the hallway. Emma had heard some banging noises, but coming out of a deep sleep, she wasn't sure what was real and what wasn't. Sometimes she woke herself out of a deep sleep with odd noises from her sinuses or even her throat that she thought were something terrible.

Clearly she couldn't be sure of anything. And yet there was a paralyzing fear keeping her from moving, from breathing normally. She couldn't even lean back for fear of the headboard creaking. What if it creaked and suddenly Abigail was in the doorway with that staring face from Emma's nightmares?

The light was slowly becoming brighter outside. Emma needed to get up and find out if anything had really happened or if, perhaps, she'd dreamt it all That would make more sense than what she thought she'd seen outside her doorway. But how to get herself to move...

She breathed in deeply, still silently at first, then more normally. Turning her body slowly perpendicular to the bed, she put on her bedroom slippers quietly and stood, putting her weight down gently and evenly on the floor. She slipped her dressing gown on, and the sound of material sliding against material seemed far too loud. She stopped to listen but heard nothing aside from her own breathing.

Emma gathered herself while she tied her dressing

gown in front. She would feel better once the bubble of fear that engulfed her room was popped. She would find Christopher immediately and ask him if he heard those strange noises last night. If he didn't...well, he was a heavy sleeper, but still. He would know if something had been amiss, Emma was sure.

She turned the doorknob but strangely, the doorknob twisted faster than she was turning it. The door pushed open and Abigail's face filled her vision, pale with blue veins, too close to her own face. A sharp gasp sprung from Emma as she stumbled backwards, claustrophobic fear stabbing her insides as they ran cold. Abigail grabbed Emma's arms tightly and Emma felt the panic of her nightmare returning so quickly she couldn't react. She wanted to yank her arms away, but they were numb suddenly and all she could do was think, *Let go, let go, let go!*

"Emma," Abigail whispered roughly. "Has Christopher already told you?"

"Ch-Christopher?" Emma barely stammered, only consonants coming out.

"Mother..." Abigail stopped for a moment, a strange expression rippling over her face and disappearing quickly.

Emma waited. When Abigail didn't speak again, Emma whispered, "What about Mother?"

The sense of urgency returned to Abigail's demeanor. "I thought I heard something last night," Abigail said, her eyes welling up. Emma distinctly noticed they were not red, though. "Something horrible happened to Mother." Abigail sobbed, but it lacked genuine sadness.

And suddenly, just like that, Emma realized why the doorknob had turned so quickly. Abigail had been waiting with her hand on the knob when Emma had tried to leave. Abigail had been waiting. She had been listening on the other side of the door and waiting.

Emma couldn't understand what Abigail was saying anymore. And she couldn't move away. Emma flashed to her nightmare, to Abigail's stolid face and the pounding fear that was now returning. Vision...her vision blurred, then flickered on and off with her heartbeat. Off balance, then a thud. Abigail's eyes so close. Too close. A last strike of paralyzing fear. Coldness. Darkness.

*

Emma had fainted before Abigail had finished telling her that Mother was dead. This was exactly why Christopher, after Abigail woke him and told him Father's story, had decided on not waking Emma to tell her. She was, as he put it, "too delicate to be woken by something so startling," so Abigail waited by her door until she heard Emma's quiet movements inside. Christopher had carried Emma downstairs to the sitting room, away from where the police were already investigating. There was a fainting couch in the room where Emma could recover. Christopher had insisted on talking to the police while Abigail took care of Emma.

Now Abigail sat with Emma laid out on the fainting couch, fanning her lightly. Emma had seemed...analytical was the only word that fit. Abigail was unsure where this left her or what it meant. It must mean Emma remembered what had happened last night. But what could she possibly know?

Abigail took a deep breath and thought logically.

Emma had not seen Mother during the incident, Abigail was sure. Emma could not have seen Mother after the

145

incident because Mother had been lying dead at the bottom of the stairs. That was certain too. The most Emma could possibly remember was her brief glimpse of Abigail against the wall, crying.

Had she heard anything? Of that, Abigail knew nothing. Well, she knew one thing, actually. Emma had most likely heard Mother's fall. That must have been what had awakened her. But Father had said it was an accident.

Emma would ask why Abigail had waited so long to get the police. Abigail was prepared to say that Father had commanded her not to say a word until morning so that he had time to escape.

He insisted, Emma. You know the kind of strained relationship they had. It was an acci—

"Abigail, are you saying something?" Emma startled her. Emma's voice was weak, but her words were clear enough. Abigail must have been mouthing the words without realizing it.

"Oh, Emma, I'm glad you're awake. How do you feel?" Abigail asked.

"Exhausted," Emma said. "I feel as if I didn't sleep at all last night." She tried to sit up, but when she propped herself up she winced and let herself fall back down onto the couch.

"You hit your head when you fainted," Abigail explained. "Christopher carried you here. We've called for a doctor."

It was only then that Emma seemed to notice the sound of footsteps going through the house. She didn't know yet that it was policemen coming in and out of the house.

Emma looked at Abigail, frightened. She rubbed her head.

Do something smart.

Abigail slunk to the floor and knelt. She took Emma's hand and held it tightly, letting her own fear of uncertainty take over so that her eyes could well up.

"Emma, did you hear what I said before you fainted?" Abigail asked, her voice quivering.

Emma shook her head.

"Mother...Mother didn't just get hurt last night," Abigail started. "Sh-she died." Pause. When she saw recognition in Emma's face of what these words meant, she continued, "Father and Mother got into a terrible fight. Did you hear it? I came out of my room just as she fell down the stairs. I couldn't believe what happened, and I was crying, and Father said he hadn't meant to, they'd just had a fight and... I'm sure he didn't mean for it to happen."

Emma stared at Abigail. This was the most Abigail had ever spoken to Emma at one time.

"Have the police taken Father?" Emma asked.

Abigail was quiet for a moment before she said, "He ran away last night. He said he knew no one would believe it was an accident."

Emma's lips parted and then closed again, nodding. "He's probably right."

"He insisted, Emma," Abigail said in a rush. "You know the kind of strained relationship—" Abigail stopped mid-sentence. Emma hadn't put up resistance like she'd expected. But now Abigail had already started explaining. She hadn't listened carefully, she'd assumed. She turned around a grabbed a piece of paper from the table behind her, putting it on Emma's stomach. "It says it all in there."

*

It took Emma a couple of long moments to realize a

folded piece of paper was lying on her stomach. She was still caught on the fact that Abigail had started to say exactly the words she'd mouthed when Emma had just woken up. Was it possible she had been practicing her explanation? What did that mean?

Now Abigail was staring at her expectantly. Emma adjusted the position of her head on the pillow to look at the paper. She picked it up and unfolded it, scanning the writing. It was a letter signed by Father. It read:

Abigail, Emma, Christopher,

I cannot apologize for my actions sincerely. I was protecting you all. Your mother was quite unwell and her understanding of reality was coming unhinged. She spoke of harming you and could not be persuaded otherwise. She attacked me and when I tried to stop her, she struggled so much that I overpowered her too greatly. She lost her balance and fell down the stairs.

Please show this to the police. Although it was an accident, I know I would be accused of her death. I also want none of you to be accused.

Your mother owned nothing legally, but I give control of my own fortune to all of you, my children. You must consider me dead. Christopher will take control of all my assets. My will says something similar, but this letter hereby gives you permission to own everything that is mine before my literal death.

Please do not worry about me. Take care of yourselves.

Your father,

Richard Whitestone

Emma looked at Abigail. "He's gone?"

And then, just this one time, Abigail's tears seemed to

flow on their own. She gasped loudly, her eyes closed, and lowered her forehead onto Emma's hand.

"At least he's alive, Abigail," Emma said, not quite able to stroke her sister's hair. Instead she gripped Abigail's hand tighter. She did feel great sympathy for her sister, someone she didn't always even consider related to herself. Mother had always treated Abigail badly, had always gone out of her way to make her own daughter miserable. Mother never liked Abigail and had never hidden that fact, but Emma had always been puzzled over why. Abigail was a quiet girl, strange with her dark-circled eyes and constant intense aura, always calculating. But their own mother should have seen past that. She did quite the opposite. Abigail had always been a tortured girl, and for that Emma felt sorry.

"Yes," Abigail said, sniffling. "At least it wasn't Father who died."

Emma frowned and gently loosened her grip.

*

One or two days was all Abigail had to wait. Father had promised. In only one or two days, he would write to her. He said to count this as the first day.

After Abigail and Emma had talked—it was the closest she'd ever been to Emma in her life—it was still only eight o'clock in the morning. By the time Christopher reached them, Abigail had let go of Emma's hand and sat next to her on the fainting couch. He looked at the letter on the table and then at Abigail. She nodded to indicate that Emma had read it.

He stared down at them, looking between them both with a solemn yet warm expression, then sat down on the table in front of them. Abigail was always taken aback a little by his lack of formality at times, though his eyes showed far more maturity than his fifteen years. He took each sister's hand in one of his own.

"We are all that's left of the Whitestones," he said. "Father will not come back. He's right; the evidence is incriminating. They think he did it on purpose."

"Are they going to look for him or leave it be?" Emma asked.

"They are going to look for him, but my impression was they wouldn't put much effort into it."

The entire town would know why; Mother was greatly disliked for not going to church, let alone her lack of social graces and decorum. Everyone thought something was wrong with her. They all knew she was wicked. The policemen must have said to each other, "Let her poor husband go but make it look good. If he comes back we'll have no choice, but just let him go."

That was how Abigail imagined it.

"We must make careful arrangements for the funeral," Christopher said.

"Careful?" Abigail asked.

"Under the circumstances, yes, careful is the best word," Christopher said. "Think of it: Mother dies—and you know the whole town will decide that Father has done it on purpose—and then he runs off the same night. We must be quite careful about how her funeral is handled. We must show some respect but also show our disapproval."

"No one will come," Abigail said. "Mother has no friends, only former acquaintances, not even current ones."

Emma flinched at this. It did not escape Abigail's notice.

"People will come," Christopher said, "for the spectacle

of it."

"Pardon me," a police constable said, knocking on the open door. All three Whitestones stood. "I'm sorry to have to ask this, but did any one of you witness the struggle indicated in Mr. Whitestone's letter? I'll need to collect that as evidence, by the way."

Emma's eyes flitted to Abigail, something Abigail knew would happen, so she immediately said, "I didn't witness the struggle itself. I woke up when I heard voices in the hall and came outside just when Mother fell."

"And neither of you heard or saw anything?" the constable asked.

"I heard her fall," Emma said. "I tried to come out into the hall to see what had happened, but Father told me Mother had had an accident and she was embarrassed about it. He told me to go back to bed."

"And did you see your sister in the hall?" the constable asked.

Emma nodded but didn't say a word. She touched her head and sat back down.

"Why didn't your father tell you to leave the hall too, Miss Whitestone?" the constable asked Abigail.

Abigail paused. She was almost sure she remembered exactly what story she'd told Emma and how it confirmed Father's letter, but what if she made a mistake? "I'd rather not say in front of my siblings."

He frowned at her. "Why not?"

"Because they were fortunate enough not to see it happen and I don't want them to suffer any more than they have to," Abigail said.

"Miss Whitestone, your siblings are aware of how Mrs. Whitestone died," he said. "I don't think much will shock them now."

Abigail took in a deep breath and exhaled in a huff. "I saw Father push Mother down the stairs."

Emma looked down and Christopher shot Abigail a surprised glance. The constable's eyebrows went up.

"You saw him push her?" he asked.

"Yes, but that's all I saw," she said.

"And you're sure of that?" he asked. "You had just woken up. You couldn't have imagined—"

"I wish I had imagined it," Abigail snapped. "I wish none of it had ever happened, but like Father's letter says, it wasn't any of our faults. Mother was a tyrant." She realized she was leaning forward and immediately pulled herself back to stand straight. She shouldn't have said that.

The constable looked off kilter now, a bit confused at her reaction, not quite sure what to make of it.

Abigail put her hand to her mouth and sobbed. She sobbed out of fear, but it looked like mourning. "I'm so tired and so upset that I saw it happen," she said, her voice breaking. "I wish I'd never heard them arguing."

"That's what caused you to come out into the hallway in the first place?" the constable asked more carefully.

"Yes," Abigail said quietly.

"And why was Mr. Whitestone allowed to leave?" the constable asked. "Didn't you try to stop him?"

Abigail's crying stopped abruptly. She dropped her hand and stared at the constable, her gaze unexpectedly hard. "Last night I witnessed a man protect his family from a mentally unstable woman. I did not witness a murder." She waited. "I let him leave."

The constable stood still for a moment, staring back at her. "I have heard rumors to the effect of... I'm sorry, Miss

Whitestone," the constable said. "I'll let you know if I have any other questions."

*

Nine o'clock in the morning. Still only nine o'clock in the morning.

Abigail paced up and down the sitting room. There were so many decisions to be made, but Abigail couldn't think of anything except hearing from Father. The thoughts were repetitive, frustrating because there was nothing Abigail could do but wait, and yet it swirled around her mind, choking out everything but pinpricks of other thoughts.

Christopher is out getting the wreath with black ribbons tied around it... What if I never hear from Father? What happens then?

That thought felt like a brick wall, like there was no living past an awful thing like that. It would be worse than the whole ordeal so far.

Invitations to the funeral must be delivered immediately. The black trim around the edges should be wide... What if they do catch Father? What will happen to him? Could I see him?

Abigail shook her head, but it didn't clear her mind.

The looking-glasses. Did Emma cover all of them?

That was one simple thing she could do, something that would allow her to leave the room where she had told Emma and Christopher and the constable lies about Mother's death. Abigail tried not to believe in things like spirits getting trapped in looking-glasses, but now that there had been a death in the house hours before they had been covered, Abigail couldn't stop fear from creeping into her heart and her stomach. Each step she took up the stairs seemed to slow her pace but speed her heartbeat. Her fingers felt colder and colder. Had Emma remembered to check Mother and Father's room for looking-glasses? Probably not...

Abigail reached the top of the stairs at the slowest pace she'd ever moved. This was the very spot where she had thrown Mother down the stairs. Everything seemed to stop. The only thing moving was her heart. All the sound of the world was silenced and there was only a deafening squeal that seemed to come from nowhere. Her vision blurred so that she could only see general shapes. Everything tilted.

Whispering.

The voices came from close behind her and startled her so deeply, she felt an unstoppable tingle that almost tickled, running from the very base of her back all the way up to her neck where it culminated in a prickle so severe it itched. But she couldn't move.

Something on her back. Something moving up next to her.

Abigail whipped her head around, uncontrolled. Her mind saw Mother's face, abnormally twisted and crinkled, smiling unnaturally wide. The devil's smile.

There was only the wallpaper. Just the stark black against white. She slammed her hand against it to make sure that was all there was next to her. That *was* all there was, but she only felt a small bit comforted.

All she had to cling to was the wall. She couldn't cry for help—she couldn't bring herself to make a sound. And if she did, what would she say when somebody reached her? She was alone in this until she heard from Father.

Abigail clung to the wall, facing it and spreading her arms out from her body as if to hug it. She flattened herself against it as much as possible and inched her way down the hall. She stopped, frowning. The texture of this wall...she had never noticed it before. She ran a finger over the black pattern and then the white. They were not just different colors, they actually *felt* different. Tracing her finger along the line of black—or was it a line of white?—focused her attention completely on the wallpaper. Her mind was clear, sharp, and everything looked highly defined, as if the black were a deep abyss and the white shone like the sun. She didn't need to cling to wallpaper. That was silly. It was a hard, tangible, non-living thing that couldn't help her. Not really. She had to walk on her own, to prove her strength of will against Mother. If Abigail should ever be unafraid of Mother, it was now. These fears had to stop now that Mother was gone. This was finally Abigail's time to live without fear.

Abigail straightened up, drawing her head up higher and her back into a taught line. Her fists clutched at the fabric of her dress, but as soon as she realized what she was doing, she forced them to stop. Taking a deep, slow breath and purposely trying to rein in her fear, Abigail walked the rest of the way down the hall to her parents' bedroom.

Mother's body had been put into a different room downstairs, where it would be easier for people to visit when the time came. Knowing that made it a little less frightening to enter Mother's room. But only a little.

Opening the door in one quick motion, Abigail stepped over the threshold but moved no farther while she looked for any looking-glasses Emma might have missed covering.

One.

There was one hanging on the wall. She suddenly realized she'd forgotten to bring a covering for the looking-glass. She stared at it, frozen in place, before she reminded herself she was still in the doorway and could just take a step back to exit the room. Sighing heavily, Abigail left the room in search of something to cover the reflective surface. There was a chest in the governess's old room with things like crepes for just such an occasion, so she got a solid black crepe from there.

When she returned to Mother's room, she paused at the threshold. *Walk in, cover the looking-glass, leave—and do it quickly.* Taking in a deep breath and holding it as if she would drown if she didn't, Abigail walked into the room as if it were any other. She didn't look into the looking-glass for fear of what she would see. If Mother's soul was trapped inside, Abigail didn't want to see it or know it. She covered the looking-glass and made sure the crepe was draped in a way that would prevent it from falling off. She stood back to look at it. Wondering if she should pin the fabric together to absolutely prevent it from falling off, Abigail reached out and smoothed a section of it down.

Something cold and wet fell on her arm. She looked at the spot and saw a single drop of water. Peering up at the ceiling didn't reveal anything wet, nothing dripping. How strange. How could... Suddenly she thought, *a teardrop.* She didn't know where the thought came from but she knew it was an odd thought and didn't make sense. There was no one in the room but her, so how could it be a teardrop?

It couldn't be...

Only a minute or two ago, Abigail had been brave, plucking up her courage to even come into the room, and yet all at once she wished she could shrink down to an inch tall and and blend in with the wooden floor. Even at an inch tall she would curl up into a ball and wait until she felt safe again—until Father was back.

If a teardrop really had fallen, it would mean Mother's spirit had stayed. It would mean Mother wasn't done with Abigail yet. It would mean that as a trapped soul, there would be no boundaries to Mother's cruelty.

Abigail felt the room getting smaller and smaller and she couldn't bear to look away from the black material in front of her.

What have I done?

*

Although nobody visited the house under normal circumstances, Abigail knew that many visitors would come to "pay their respects" and view the body. They might even go so far as offering to help with the arrangements even though what they really wanted, Abigail knew, was to satisfy their curiosity, to see as much of the house as possible where such an unspeakable thing had happened. Murder was what they all would suspect, that morbid thing that was always a source of fascination to everyone. They would want a glance inside the Whitestone walls with the hopes of spotting something obviously wicked—a spot of blood, a look between the sisters, the letter Father had left. As if anyone would be stupid enough to let any of that be seen.

After the police had taken their notes earlier in the day, they allowed the area to be cleaned. Abigail had gotten down on her hands and knees and scrubbed Mother's blood off the softwood floor with a stiff brush and an alkaline solution. The servants had not even offered to do it for her. Instead they stood where they thought they couldn't be seen, but Abigail saw them perfectly well. Staring.

Watching her scrub in her black dress where Mother's head had hit the floor so hard the blood was still wet; there was so much it couldn't dry completely over the course of several hours.

Somehow it didn't disgust her to cleanse the floor of Mother's blood. She was obsessive about it, scrubbing so hard her arm hurt, yet it felt good. The kind of pain that was also relief, and so she needed to keep going even after the blood was gone. Abigail scrubbed at the bloodstain that had dyed the wood until Christopher's shoes came into view next to her. He knelt down, put his hand on her shoulder and said, "I think it's enough now, Abigail. We'll have to get a floorcloth to cover the stain."

She kept scrubbing.

"Abigail," he whispered very close to her ear, "it's too much. The servants are asking if they should call a doctor. They think something…more is wrong with you."

She stopped and put both hands on the brush, leaning all her weight on it. "And how is one supposed to act when scrubbing their parent's blood off the floor?" She looked at him and could feel a harshness in her gaze she had never expressed toward him before. She hadn't meant it, but she couldn't stop it either.

Christopher frowned slowly, moving his head away from hers. More than surprise, his eyes held a look of disappointment. He'd reached out to help her and she'd practically smacked his hand. Suddenly Abigail's heart felt like it was developing a hole.

Before she could say anything, Christopher yanked the brush from her hand and picked up the pail of water. He walked toward the kitchen, probably to spill the reddened water out back behind the house. Abigail plopped herself down on the floor from her kneeling position. She ran her finger along the soaked grains of wood. She had damaged it a bit with all her hard scrubbing. She'd only wanted to clean it, but it couldn't be cleaned. It could never be cleaned.

*

Abigail stayed in her room for the rest of the day, overwhelmed with regret about how she'd treated Christopher and worry about Father, about when his letter would come. Over the course of an hour, Father had completely taken over her thoughts, and her stomach jumped every few minutes. Her heart felt as if it were on a cliff, waiting for the fragile edge to give out below the weight of such intense anxieties, sending her heart plummeting to the deathly jagged, feared outcome below. If Father didn't write, she didn't know what she would do. Whatever it was, she was afraid of that too. She didn't feel she had any real control over herself. Her feelings, her… reaction to Mother, to Christopher. What would she do next? She couldn't lose control anymore. She had to be able to rely on her own sense of security, and nothing—and nobody—else. That would bring her strength.

She didn't have her Bible anymore. Mother had disposed of it so that Abigail couldn't even find it in the refuse, nor were there any traces of it burned in the fireplaces. But she remembered one quote in particular very well and recited it: "The Lord is on my side; I will not fear: what can man do unto me? The Lord is on my side; I will not fear: what can man do unto me?"

*

Abigail slept on and off throughout the day, going downstairs only when she thought the evening mail might have come. Each time she'd been wrong, but finally she was right. Emma had gotten to it first and was sorting it out. If Father's letter was in there, Emma would know his handwriting even if he didn't include his return address.

Emma looked up when she realized Abigail was standing near her, waiting. Neither sister said a word, but Emma was clearly uncomfortable. Abigail couldn't ask if there was anything for her because there never was, so it would seem too odd. She hadn't planned what she would do in a case like this. Her anxieties were getting the better of her.

"I...thought I might use your *Godey's Lady's Book* to take my mind off of everything," Abigail lied. It was so out of character for her that Emma clutched the mail close to her chest and squinted at Abigail.

"Why did you wait to tell me about Mother?" Emma asked, surprising Abigail.

"What do you mean? I told you right after I told Christopher," Abigail said.

"You waited for me to wake up," Emma said. "You woke *Christopher* right away. Why didn't you wake me too? Even before him?"

"He knew it would be the last time you slept well for a long time," Abigail said, putting the blame on him. It had been his idea to wait, after all. What was Emma playing at? "He didn't want to shock you awake."

Emma shook her head. "I came out of my room last night to ask if everything was all right. You and Father both could have told me then. Or you could have come to me right after Father left. Of course I'd still be awake, he couldn't have taken that long to leave. It makes no sense."

Abigail moved up to Emma in one big step, putting

herself only a couple of inches away from her sister. Then she fingered a curl of Emma's strawberry-blonde hair on the side of her head, pulling at it a little too much. She looked Emma in the eyes, standing taller than her sister.

"I would watch what I ask, if I were you," Abigail said quietly. "I can't protect you if you won't let me."

Emma's eyes grew so wide and round they looked like targets. "F-from what?" she asked.

Abigail tugged at the hair harder, then let it go. "Curiosity…" she said. She put her hand out, indicating to Emma that she should complete the sentence.

Emma stared at her, blinking.

"Say it," Abigail said flatly.

"Killed the cat?" Emma asked.

Abigail held her hand out for the mail, not breaking eye contact. Emma handed it to her without hesitation. Abigail took her time looking through what little mail there was, even though the magazine stood out. She looked Emma in the eye again unwaveringly while she put the mail down on the table next to the door instead of handing it back to Emma, keeping the magazine in her arms.

"Don't forget," Abigail whispered. She turned around and walked away. Perhaps Emma would think twice before asking probing questions again. Perhaps Emma would think twice before talking to Christopher behind Abigail's back, like she clearly had.

As she climbed the stairs, her heart swelled with…was this what power felt like? Was this how Mother had always felt through her cruelty? But Abigail wasn't Mother. She always had a good reason to act the way she did. She was not unprovoked. She was not cruel. She was different.

September 15, 1860

Abigail sat in the parlor from five in the morning the next day, waiting for the morning mail. Next to her on the couch, she kept the book Conrad had given her along with her embroidery. It was not unusual for Abigail to stay home all day, but it was unusual for her to sit in the same place for hours at a time.

Picking up *The Black Tulip*, Abigail opened it to the page where she'd left a black ribbon. There was such an unusual and interesting quote that she had to read it again:

"To despise flowers is to offend God. The more beautiful the flower is, the more does one offend God in despising it. The tulip is the most beautiful of all flowers. Therefore, he who despises the tulip offends God beyond measure."

Part of that might go nicely on a pillow for her room, perhaps just the first sentence. Perhaps she could find some lovely tulips to put in the front hall when it was finally appropriate after mourning.

She laid the book down and realized she hadn't heard from Conrad since Mother's death. Not a letter, not a visit, no flowers. Nothing.

Perhaps he was being a gentleman and letting her mourn for a little while. It was, after all, only the second day after Mother's death. She didn't know the rules of mourning when it came to a suitor, and she wasn't about to ask her siblings. She would be patient. If any man knew the rules of society, it was Conrad. He would know what was best.

Abigail continued reading, and in another few pages she came across another quite true quote:

"But to kill a tulip was a horrible crime in the eyes of a genuine tulip-fancier; as to killing a man, it would not have mattered so very much."

She thought of Mother throwing her flowers away. In fact she had done more than throw them away. Abigail had found them outside the back door scattered among the trash and cut into tiny pieces. It had nearly made her cry—until she'd remembered Mother was gone, and there was no need to worry about that ever happening again. Then her building tears had dissipated quickly.

There was no bad side Abigail could think of—aside from Father's absence—to Mother's death. Perhaps the others thought of it differently. Mother had always treated them better. But still, they had to see what poison she was.

One thought suddenly broke across all others and sat heavily in the center of her mind. Did Mother know of Emma's romance with Mr. Pendlebury? And did they speak of it together? Most of Abigail's days revolved around avoiding Mother, so she wouldn't have noticed if there was more of a closeness between them than she'd known.

It shouldn't have bothered her. Even if their relationship was warm and wonderful, they couldn't have it anymore. Not ever again.

Abigail realized she'd been reading without seeing the words for quite some time, quite a few pages, and now her eyes blankly read the same line over and over again. She stopped, focused, and reread it, giving it her full attention:

"But there is this terrible thing in evil thoughts, that evil minds soon grow familiar with them."

She put her ribbon in the book and set it down.

*

There had been nothing in the morning mail, which

Abigail noticed Emma never came to look through. Abigail fretted. Father had promised he would send a letter in only one or two days. He'd *promised.* Abigail had little experience with his promises and whether or not he usually kept them, but she had expected he was a man of his word. Could she have been wrong?

Or...perhaps he would send a letter this evening and it would reach her the next morning. That made perfect sense. So if there was nothing in the evening mail, it wouldn't make a difference to her, she decided.

But it did make a difference. All day long Abigail sat with her embroidery and mostly ran the threads between her fingertips over and over and over. She couldn't concentrate well enough to stitch anything. The same worries about Father ran through her head until they felt irritating, like scratching an itch until the skin bled. Her mind bled with anxiety. Time was slow and she did nothing to try to speed it up.

Emma went out. Christopher went out. Christopher came back. Lunch was served. Emma came back and ate lunch late. Abigail didn't notice the food she ate. Later, she didn't remember whether she had eaten anything at all. After lunch Emma went upstairs. Christopher sat in the sitting room with Abigail. Abigail pretended to read, and although she turned the pages of her book, she never removed the ribbon from her starting page; when she put the book down, the ribbon remained where it had started. Emma came in for afternoon tea. As soon as she sat down, Abigail said she wasn't feeling well and went upstairs. She hoped to fall asleep and wake up in time for the mail to arrive. But she couldn't even keep her eyes closed.

It was an odd balance of time. Each activity seemed

sudden and immediate when it happened, but the time in between dragged as if it wasn't moving at all. It felt like days before the grandfather clock would strike the next hour. There could be nothing more miserable than waiting. Bland, tense waiting.

*

The evening mail arrived just after Abigail had come downstairs again. Emma and Christopher were in the parlor, so she took it and sat down in a chair in the dining room.

She stared down at the first envelope. A bill. As she took the envelope between her fingers to move it to the back of the very small pile, Abigail hesitated. Her hands were sweaty. She'd gone over it many times in her head by now: *if Father's letter isn't here, it will be in tomorrow morning's mail.* And yet she felt this was the end, the final word on whether he would write to her.

Raising the envelope slightly above the others, she peeked at the handwriting on the next one. It was not Father's.

Abigail's spine tingled.

"Miss Whitestone," came the maid's voice loudly from beside her.

Abigail jumped in her seat and glared up at the maid. "What?" she said harshly.

"I'm sorry to have frightened you," Ashdon said. "I just wondered if you wanted dinner served early since you're sitting at the table. I thought you might—"

"No, no, the usual time will be fine," Abigail said.

"Of course, miss," Ashdon said. "Would you like me to sort the mail for you?"

"No, I will do it myself," she said impatiently.

Ashdon nodded before she walked away.

Abigail stared back down at the envelopes. She couldn't take this slow torture anymore. She quickly dealt them out on the table like playing cards and looked from one to the next.

None of them were from Father.

Abigail's heart pounded in her chest and deafened her panicked thoughts.

Tomorrow, tomorrow, she kept forcing herself to think, but she didn't believe herself. She still didn't understand why he didn't write. He had gone through all the trouble to help her, to take the blame on himself and destroy his reputation. He'd even seemed to understand how she had suffered throughout her life. But perhaps he hadn't really done it for her. Perhaps he had wanted to escape and this was just the means by which to do it.

He hadn't helped her. He had used her.

And yet, her crushing disappointment turned inward. There was only one thing she could think. Something was wrong with her. Something had always been wrong with her. It must have been there from the day she was born and it had followed her, sticking to her very essence, all the way up through today. She just didn't know what it was. And that—that lack of understanding, that missing piece—was what caused the deepest rupture in her heart.

*

Abigail put the mail on the table by the front door. She felt cold all over and damp at the same time.

"Well," she heard Christopher say to Emma in the parlor, "I'd never have imagined something like that happening here."

Abigail looked toward the parlor but didn't move.

"Mother always hated Mrs. Hinsley," Emma said. "She never treated me poorly, but Mother always hated her. I don't know why."

"I suppose we should send Mr. Hinsley something or visit him. A visit might be nicer," Christopher said. "It's so rare anyone goes missing. And it's been two days. He must be so worried."

"And lonely," Emma added.

Abigail didn't hear any more of their words. All she could hear was blood pounding inside her ears. She walked swiftly to her room, using all her strength, which was fading rapidly. Her breath was shallow and she couldn't take in the amount of air her lungs needed. Toward the top of the stairs, she almost felt she wouldn't make it. She stood there, her foot partially raised but not enough to clear the stair. She looked at her door and concentrated on what would happen if she fainted now. She would join Mother in the same death.

After climbing the last step, Abigail couldn't straighten her knee. She tripped over her dress and fell to her knees hard. She vaguely heard air rasping, struggling to get through her closing windpipe. She crawled the rest of the way to her room and shut the door. As soon as she had locked it, still on her knees, she collapsed in a curled-up ball on the hard wood floor, her arms using all their strength to keep her knees to her chest, her eyes buried in them. Her dress absorbed her tears.

Mrs. Hinsley was missing, had been for two days. Father had gone away with her. Of course he had, this was his own chance for happiness. And now he didn't care about Abigail. He had chosen Mrs. Hinsley instead, and Abigail had nothing to do with his happiness. His daughter's own need for him was not his concern. He didn't care. He didn't love her. No one did.

The pain seared through her entire body and she could no longer hold it inside. She put her open mouth to her knee and howled her agony through her dress. The noise was quieted but not silent, but she couldn't think about what her siblings might hear, and if either of them knocked on her door, she didn't notice. She cried hard for an amount of time she couldn't count, her face blazing hot, her eyes shut and swollen. And through it all, she had only one thought.

I was not made to be loved.

September 16, 1860

The next day, Abigail came downstairs quite late after refusing breakfast in bed from Ashdon. What the maid didn't know was that she'd never made it to bed; she'd slept in her curled-up position on the floor all night. She was deathly pale and her eyes were still red. She made no effort to hide her wretched appearance. She hadn't even redone her hair, leaving it frizzy and messy in its style from the previous day.

"Oh," she heard Emma say in surprise at her appearance when she reached the first floor.

Abigail looked at her but said nothing.

"What on earth happened, Abigail? Are you sick? You should have told Ashdon."

Abigail still said nothing and started to walk aimlessly toward the dining room even though she wasn't hungry and wasn't going to eat.

"Abigail?" Still no response. Emma continued, "There are some flowers for you by the front door."

Abigail stopped walking and turned around. "Flowers?" Her voice was rough.

Emma tilted her head as if Abigail was shorter than her. "Yes, in a box." When Abigail finally focused her eyes on Emma, she could see that Emma had a small smile. "Perhaps they're from Mr. Scott?" she suggested gently.

Abigail's heart jumped a little.

"Perhaps," she said and walked to the table by the front door, moving faster as she got closer. It was a long white box with a black ribbon around it. She hoped they were calla lilies. It would be perfect.

Abigail brought the box into the parlor and sat down on

the couch with it. Emma sat next to her, smiling bigger now.

"It's so nice to have something happy around here," Emma said, tapping the flower box.

Abigail smiled a little too. She wiggled the ribbon off the slim width of the box and then pulled it down the length of the box. She opened the lid and tossed it on the floor.

Emma gasped.

Inside were bright yellow Indian Cress with red in the middle, almost overshadowed by the overwhelming amount of Amaranthus, better known as love-lies-bleeding. This was a bouquet to free Conrad from her. Indian Cress meant resignation.

Abigail was surprised to feel Emma's arm around her.

"I'm so sorry, Abigail," Emma said, and she sounded it.

A drop of water hit the stem of an Amaranthus flower. It must have been from Abigail, but she hadn't felt the tear leave her eye.

Emma reached her fingers between the stems and pulled out a small card Abigail hadn't spotted.

"You open it," Abigail said. Her fingers trembled so that she couldn't have read it if she'd tried. She couldn't even look at Emma, couldn't watch her lips read the words.

"Are you sure?" Emma whispered.

Abigail nodded softly.

"It says, 'There is nothing I can do. The scandal is too much. I will not forget you.'"

She could feel Emma's eyes on her and feel her shoulder being rubbed.

"What scandal?" Emma asked.

Abigail sniffed. This confirmed it. And the entire town must have known. But this time, no more tears escaped her eyes. She felt as if the pain from yesterday was hardening into something icy, heavy, something she wished she could cut out of her but knew she couldn't. She was surprised to find she couldn't feel much of anything anymore.

"I don't want to ruin your memories of Father," Abigail said softly. "All I will tell you is that we will both have trouble finding husbands now."

Part 2

*For I have eaten ashes like bread, and mingled my drink
with weeping, because of thine indignation and thy wrath:
for thou hast lifted me up, and cast me down.*

Psalm 102:9–10
King James Bible

20–21 years old
1860–1861

September 27, 1860

ELIZABETH WHITESTONE.
Died 13th September 1860, aged 41 years.
"The LORD is nigh unto them that are of a broken heart;
and saveth such as be of a contrite spirit."
—PSALM 34:18

This was Mother's epitaph. The slate tombstone had a simple piece of art, something ironic: an engraved Bible. She was dead, and there was nothing more to say, and certainly nothing more that she deserved.

Abigail stood by the grave two weeks after Conrad's flowers had arrived. She'd felt a strong pull to visit Mother, though she didn't know why. She had nothing to say.

Abigail put down the bouquet of orange lilies and pheasant's eye flowers held together by dodder vine. It was a bouquet of hatred, and if anyone bothered to visit, they'd know that. But she didn't care what people thought anymore. This was between her and Mother. *Mother.* The name didn't sound right anymore. It never really had.

Kneeling down, Abigail lowered herself slowly, leaning on one hand as she rolled into a lying position atop the grave. She picked up the bouquet and held it in one hand, letting it rest lightly between her arm and her body. Her eyes remained wide, staring off beyond the sky. One by one, she absent-mindedly plucked flower petals off the pheasant's eyes, letting each one drop from her fingers and blow away in the wind.

She recalled her conversation with Mr. Hinsley when she'd visited him a week after Mrs. Hinsley's disappearance. Even though it was unacceptable socially for a lady to visit a gentleman, she'd thought it would be worth breaking this rule. What had she to lose anyway? She'd thought they could talk and share their misery of both people who meant so much to them leaving abruptly for each other. She thought it was something easy to bond over. Perhaps for once she could share her pain with someone, just once.

Mr. Hinsley had been gaunt, just as Abigail still was. It was hard to say nice things about Mrs. Hinsley, not only because she had abandoned her husband, and not only because she had abandoned her husband for Abigail's own father, making Abigail feel somehow responsible for both their losses. It was also hard because Mrs. Hinsley had been so kind to Abigail, the only real semblance of a mother to her, and yet she had done this revolting thing. Abigail's feelings of disgust were so strong, she almost didn't know how to say Mrs. Hinsley's name, as if it were hard to pronounce.

Mr. Hinsley and Abigail had another thing in common: public shame. Everyone knew of the affair now, and they reveled in it, Abigail was sure. The filthy words that must have passed from mouth to mouth made her cringe every time it entered her mind. And it entered more frequently than she could control. It was humiliating to them both.

They had sat in silence for quite some time after the usual pleasantries, if you could call them that. Mr. Hinsley held Mrs. Hinsley's cameo in his hands, the one that looked exactly like her, and rubbed it with his thumb. It was almost mesmerizing to watch, until he said quite out of the blue, "She even took the bird with her."

"What?" Abigail asked.

"The bird. There was a bird—your late mother gave Victoria the cage—and she took that too." He sounded on the verge of tears, which Abigail hadn't expected. "They have the bird with them too."

Abigail had opened her mouth to say something, try to comfort him, but he said abruptly, "Please go. I'm sorry to be rude, but your presence is making this worse. It's not your fault, of course. I would just like you to go, please."

And so Abigail had stood awkwardly, looked him up and down slowly, waiting for him to change his mind, and when he didn't, she left. The rest of the day Abigail had felt as if she were standing at an angle. Even the one person who could sympathize with her wouldn't help her. He couldn't even help himself.

Blinking herself out of the memory, Abigail got up off the grave and left. All that remained of the bouquet on the grave was vines wrapped around stems.

October 3, 1860

Abigail, Emma, and Christopher convened in the sitting room facing each other. Each was on a different piece of furniture. Abigail sat in an oversized armchair of dark wood and deep red, uncomfortable cushions. Emma sat alone in the middle of the long couch and Christopher sat in another armchair, one of normal proportion that had a beautiful pattern and soft cushions.

"The inheritance from our parents," Abigail started slowly, "is in your hands, Christopher." She waited a moment, staring at him with unblinking eyes. "That's what Father asked for. But you're still quite young. "

"Young, but Father showed me how to pay bills and how to keep ledgers," Christopher said. He didn't sound offended, simply matter of fact.

"Good," Abigail said. "But…there is still the matter of Emma's eventual marriage, your eventual marriage, maintaining our current social positions in such a way that will attract a husband and a wife for each of you. Those things are more natural to a woman."

"I wouldn't say—" Christopher began, but Abigail interrupted.

"Of course you're the only male child, the heir, as it were, but you're so young. And there's Emma. You should both be able to live your lives as free of cares and responsibilities as possible until you go off on your own. You should live your lives as if our parents were still here. It wouldn't be fair to put such a strain on you, Christopher, as to ask you to make your own marriage by yourself and, even more importantly, make Emma's." Abigail let that sink in. When his frown was fully formed and his eyes were on the ground, she continued, "It's not that you're incapable, Christopher, it's just that you'd be responsible if you handled it wrong, and, well…I think that's unfair. I'm the eldest. And I'd rather act as a parent to you both than in my own selfish interest."

Christopher processed this argument.

"After all, I can dedicate myself to such matters. Neither of you can do that. You're still solidifying your places in society."

"I'm not sure this would go over well with a future wife," Christopher said. "I appreciate your selflessness, Abigail, but I really do think—"

"Your happiness and your future mean so much to me," Abigail insisted, looking between her two siblings and leaning forward. "I just want the chance to make your lives normal. I don't want you to worry about a household that should, from your perspective, work unseen and unheard."

Christopher's elbows were on his knees as he rubbed his head with all the fingers of both hands. "What do you think, Emma?"

Emma looked at Abigail and lingered on her focused eyes before looking back to Christopher and answering cautiously, "I don't think any one of us should have to take on the burden of an entire estate. I think we should share it."

"You need to focus on the social aspect of your life, on securing a suitable husband," said Abigail.

"You are four years older than I, Abigail, so it's even more important for you to do both those things. Really we both need to focus on social obligations, so it makes the most sense to split all the responsibilities equally."

"Yes, it's only fair, Abigail," Christopher said, sounding

resolved to his decision. "And if anyone should take on extra responsibilities, it should be me. I'll be running this house myself someday soon anyway. I should learn everything Father would have taught me."

"My reputation has always been very low as I was never taught the social graces you were. That left me plenty more time than you to learn how to run a house, something I hoped I wouldn't need to do this soon," Abigail said, but her tone didn't match her words. It sounded like the smooth coldness of steel. "It's not a matter of opinion. With the reason and the way my courtship was ended so publicly, and of course Mother... I'm not a wanted guest in most homes. But you two have always been accepted in circles I wasn't. Over time, others may simply sympathize with you, but they won't ostracize you. The truth is..." a pause, "Mother loved you." Christopher's mouth opened, but Abigail quickly silenced him with a finger in the air. "There's no reason it shouldn't be said aloud. Mother never favored me. I've had to pay the price for that with no outside friends, just my sister and brother, so it's easy for others to shun me completely now. Since you are the only two I have in the world now, let me take care of you. I think it makes the most sense to set you both up in the world properly since you're both in good positions."

Christopher looked worried.

"Don't think twice about it, Christopher, you can look in on everything I do. But it's best this way." Abigail sat back in the chair. "And anyway, it will give me a purpose. Otherwise, I wouldn't be surprised if your future wife starts to resent me for doing nothing but reading."

At that Christopher laughed in a push of air out of his nose and a closed-mouth smile. Emma said nothing.

October 5, 1860

Abigail lay on her bed and stared at the ceiling, unblinking. She had to lead her brother and sister through life now, at least for a couple more years. And then Emma would leave her and she would be nothing more than something in the way to Christopher and his future wife. She would be the same as she always was—an unwanted extra. She couldn't explain why she needed to stay here instead of trying to find a husband and move out, or even instead of traveling for a while. She couldn't understand her attachment. It was a clawing need, something urgent and constant. But why?

It would be so much nicer for everyone if they all just stayed put in this house where they belonged. It would be so nice.

Abigail rolled over onto her side and opened the drawer in her bedside table. Out of it, she took Mother's engagement ring. She moved onto her back again and held the ring up, pinching it between her forefinger and thumb. The silver still looked new, the three rose-cut diamonds brilliant even in dull lamp light. The diamonds lay in the middle of delicate scroll filigree. Abigail touched her finger to each diamond. It was almost as if one was for Emma, one was for Christopher, and the middle one was for her, as if it was meant for Abigail to wear.

Abigail slipped the ring onto her left ring finger, laid both arms straight by her sides, and closed her eyes. She slept soundly for twelve hours, deep and undisturbed by the knocks on her door. She didn't move once.

October 8, 1860

Abigail eased the door of Mother's room open and peered inside. Somehow it surprised her that it looked the same as when she had gone in to cover the looking-glass. Thankfully it was still covered and would stay that way. Abigail was afraid to take it off.

She tiptoed in as if someone was sleeping inside and closed the door behind her softly. She wanted to look through everything in the room and decide what to keep and what to give away. Perhaps she could even find a thing or two to give her a better understanding of her parents. Wouldn't that be nice.

Although Abigail's intentions were clear to herself and the looking-glass was covered, she found she couldn't bring herself to move farther into the room. She felt nailed to the spot by a physical heaviness she couldn't describe. She also felt watched, probably just because this wasn't her room. Perhaps also because one of her parents wasn't dead and the other's essence would remain forever. The latter was a frightening concept, but Abigail knew better than to think Mother would depart from the house permanently.

Nevertheless, these things had to be gone through by someone. At least that's what she told herself to justify her rummaging.

She couldn't bring herself to say it out loud, but in her head she repeated, "Be of good courage, and He shall strengthen your heart, all ye that hope in the Lord." Somehow she'd thought the darkness of the room would lift with that quote, but it didn't. Holding her breath, Abigail walked to the two windows in the room and flung the heavy brown drapes wide to let the sun in. That certainly helped with the darkness. Not so much with the heaviness.

Now Abigail didn't know where to start. How could she ease herself into this? Perhaps with clothing. That would be simple enough.

Abigail opened the carved mahogany armoire that contained Mother's dresses. She already knew Father's things would be gone, but still, the emptiness of the armoire on his side seemed strange, regardless of the fact that she'd never looked inside before.

Mother's dresses were plain and simple but still attractive. Not very many colors but they were tasteful. If Abigail could break the association with Mother, she would quite like them. Yes, she could really like them.

There was material bunched up at the bottom of the armoire, something in a pile, it looked like. Abigail bent to pick up the clothing and found it was a dress of pale green. A wedding dress. This must have been Mother's. She was surprised that Mother still had it, even if it had been crumpled on the floor of the armoire like trash. Perhaps she had saved it for Emma. *Certainly not for me*, Abigail thought and felt a darkening feeling creep through her brain. Kept for Emma, Abigail was sure now. The more she ran the idea through her mind, the more positive she became until it was a fact to her. *A dress for Emma, not for me*, over and over it repeated. Well then, that would have to be fixed, wouldn't it?

Abigail gathered all the dresses except the wedding dress and took them to her room. The wedding dress remained alone in the armoire, abandoned on its floor again, crumpled but not forgotten. Anything but forgotten.

October 9, 1860

Abigail sat at the head of the table for all meals now, assuming her role as mistress of the house. It didn't feel unnatural to her, and in fact it even felt natural to tell their cook what she wanted made if her idea differed from their usual weekly meals. She had asked for a special meal tonight during which she could tell Christopher and Emma something important. If it worked, it would solidify her place, although she'd already sewn that up quite tightly.

Supper was to be a first course of asparagus soup followed by a second course of beef olives and salad with a third course of pickled smelts and stewed mushrooms. Dessert would be small plum cakes and dried fruits. It was a bit much for an everyday meal, but Christopher would love it.

Abigail was already seated at the dining room table when Emma and Christopher came in. They sat on either side of her in their usual places—Emma to her right, Christopher on her left—which hadn't changed since their parents were no longer there. The only thing that had changed was Abigail moving to the top of the table.

"I have a special supper planned tonight," Abigail said. "I thought it would make a nice change."

"That's nice," Christopher said. "What are we having?"

"You'll see," Abigail said, "but it's some things we haven't had in quite some time."

Christopher smiled. "Mother's ring looks well on you," he said, inclining his head toward her left hand.

Emma said nothing.

"I was surprised to find it fits perfectly," Abigail said.

"On your left hand it looks like you're engaged,

though," he said. "Shouldn't you wear it on your right hand?"

Abigail paused. "I don't think I'd like to try again after Mr. Scott."

"You're too young to say that," Christopher said but pursued it no further. Probably because he knew it wasn't true. At nearly twenty-one years old, Abigail was not so young in terms of marriage. But there was something else besides optimism in Christopher's response. There was a confirmation that clicked in her head. Abigail hadn't told Christopher about Mr. Scott. Emma must have told him what happened. They were always talking, those two. It was an odd sort of distance between them and her. And yet Christopher acted no differently toward Abigail than he did toward Emma, it seemed. Emma was the sticking point. Abigail was sure of it.

The asparagus soup was served.

"I had this at a dinner party once," Christopher said. "It was wonderful. I'm glad you thought to have it here, Abigail. Something different never hurt anyone."

"It doesn't, does it?" Abigail said. "Emma, have you had this soup before?"

"No," Emma said. "It's quite unusual."

"It's good to try new things, Emma," Abigail said.

"It is," Christopher said, glancing up at Emma.

Emma, once again, said nothing.

"You know, I've been thinking," Abigail said. "We have so much to be thankful for. We shouldn't be so selfish as to keep it all." Abigail waited before continuing and gauged the reaction around the table. Nothing from either of them yet. "Wouldn't it be nice if we helped the church in some way? After all, a lot of people came to visit us after Mother passed away even though she didn't attend church anymore."

"That's true, I was surprised how many people came to help arrange the funeral," Christopher said. "That's a nice idea, Abigail." He took a spoonful of soup. "What do you think, Emma?"

"How can it be wrong?" she said. It wasn't really an answer, just a neutral statement. Abigail recognized that.

"Did you have something specific in mind, Abigail?" Christopher asked.

"Well, I know the Bibles need replacing. Many of them are damaged. Of course they've been around for quite some time. I thought it might be especially nice to replace them," Abigail said.

The empty soup bowls were taken off the table.

"Mmm, I do love a good start to supper," Christopher said, smiling. "That does sound like a nice idea. It would be quite a help to them, don't you think, Emma?"

"Of course it would," Emma said. "Have you spoken to anyone in the church about this yet, Abigail?" When speaking to Abigail, suspicion was becoming a natural inflection in Emma's voice.

"Why would I do that when I hadn't consulted my family yet?" Abigail said.

The next course was served and the conversation remained on hold until everyone had full plates.

"You've really picked good dishes tonight, Abigail," Christopher said. "Good food makes a man feel reborn."

"I think it's very important," Abigail said. "Nourishment doesn't have to be boring."

Emma seemed to be making an effort to stay out of the entire conversation unless directly addressed.

"I thought we could reserve one of the better pews for ourselves," Abigail said. "That works to both the church's and our advantage."

"Why do we need a better pew?" Christopher asked. "I'm happy with where we sit now."

"Don't you think it's very awkward to sit next to Mr. Hinsley since Father left?" Abigail asked. This was another subject she didn't know if Emma had broached with Christopher. "He hasn't come back to church yet since Mrs. Hinsley went missing, but it could cause a problem when he returns." She took a bite of beef. "And besides, now that we have only each other and no one else to speak for us, we should really make an effort to show our worth. We could improve our reputation in a charitable way."

"They're expensive, aren't they," Emma said. "Couldn't we save that money for something more useful?"

"It could go toward your dowry," Abigail said. "When you marry, your husband would own it. Well, except for Christopher's portion, I suppose."

"It would look good to future spouses," Christopher said as his plate was cleared. "It could help us meet people we wouldn't meet otherwise. Especially since Father can no longer introduce us. We need a means to meet other families properly."

"It just seems to me," Emma said, "that we could save the expense—and it is an expense—and use it in a more sensible way. And is it really appropriate to spend so much money in such an obvious way when we're still in full mourning?"

"We just won't go too far on buying ornate pillows and rugs for our pew," Christopher said, his eyes focused on the next course being served to him. "It might even show that through this horrible time we have become even more pious."

"No one will think that," Emma said quietly.

This time, Abigail said nothing. Christopher was fighting her battle for her. Sweet Christopher.

"I think it's a fine idea, Abigail," Christopher said. "I'll speak to someone about it this Sunday."

And they hadn't even reached dessert yet.

*

Emma concentrated on her needlework while Christopher read the evening newspaper. Abigail was nowhere in sight, but Emma had something on her mind she couldn't risk Abigail hearing. It was late enough now that the kitchen staff was no longer on duty. Abigail never went into the kitchen, so this was the time to get Christopher alone there. Emma knew Abigail was very good at keeping quiet and listening, so she couldn't outright ask Christopher to go into the kitchen with her.

"The plum cake was wonderful tonight, wasn't it, Christopher?" Emma asked.

He took a moment before he looked up and nodded his head. He'd started to look down again but then glanced up and said, "You know, I could just fit another slice, too." Food always interested Christopher. "I'll ring for Ashdon."

She had to get him into the kitchen. How could she get him there without asking out loud? Whispering would make her seem mad.

"No, no," she said quickly. "You can't ask Ashdon. It's improper to eat after dinner."

"Of course," he said, clearly disappointed. "I will ask the cook to make another tomorrow."

She exhaled impatiently. "We could go get it

ourselves," she said. "There will be some left for the servants. We could just take two slices—they won't miss them."

He raised his eyebrows at her. "I'm sure they will," he said.

"Well, just one slice then, and we can share it."

He smiled. "I suppose we're both improper then," he said and stood.

Finally.

She followed him to the kitchen; the walk seemed much longer than it ever was before. She kept looking back at the staircase, expecting to see Abigail's eyes gleaming over an oil lamp, but instead she just saw darkness.

Christopher held the door for her and she walked through, making sure the door was closed after he came in.

"You can't make a habit out of this," Christopher said. "Your future husband won't like it."

"Neither will your future wife," Emma said. "Christopher, I'm concerned about our money."

He frowned, looking around the kitchen. "Where's the cake?"

"I don't know," she said, "I really just wanted to speak with you alone."

"Why not in the parlor?" he asked, still looking around a bit.

"Not where Abigail can hear," she said more quietly.

He frowned slightly. "What about our money? Abigail mostly handles it, so if you want—"

"That's exactly it," she said. "She's trying to spend it in large quantities lately on things we don't need. You should be checking how much she's spending. She isn't even asking for your approval."

"Why should she? It's her money as much as yours and mine."

Emma's lips straightened into the balance line she wished her brother would pay attention to. "It's not, actually. Don't you remember Father's letter? *You* are to take control of all our assets, not Abigail."

"Yes, but we settled all this recently," he said, sounding a little annoyed. "Abigail will take care of everything. She has sacrificed her own life to make ours better, Emma. It would be tantamount to a slap in the face to ask to check on the way she's taking care of us."

"She said it herself, you know. Remember? She said you could look in on the figures any time."

Christopher inhaled deeply, then said, "Yes, but stop thinking of it from a monetary perspective. Think of it from an individual's perspective. Abigail will be hurt if I question her. And besides, she always has a good reason, if not a kind reason, for doing what she does."

Emma's face reddened. "Kind?" she asked. That word. It was inexcusable. But Christopher didn't know the way Abigail treated Emma behind his back. She was... frightening. That was the only word to describe it. Emma couldn't check on the finances herself—Abigail would do something horrible. But if Christopher checked...

She couldn't believe he'd used the word "kind" to describe Abigail. But then again, as far as Emma knew, Christopher had never suffered Abigail's blunted threats. Emma felt powerless in the face of them. Now Emma needed to get Christopher on her side so that when Abigail did something horrible—what, Emma didn't know, but this all had to be building toward something—Christopher felt sympathy for *Emma*. Right now, his sympathy leaned toward Abigail. It disgusted Emma, how easily Abigail could manipulate. Sometimes Emma felt disgusted by herself and her lack of ability to stand up for herself. But she was scared. She was afraid she would suffer the same awful fate as Mother. Emma wasn't stupid. She'd listened hard and was sure she'd heard the constables say Mother's neck broke and her skull cracked when she fell down the steps. They'd said it hadn't just been an accident. For her to fall so that her skull had fractured, she had to be pushed hard, completely off balance. But they assumed it was Father. The note, the talk around town of their relationship, everything pointed to him. But it didn't add up. Father was quiet. Sometimes he could even make Mother stop when she was too harsh with Abigail. He wouldn't have done something so unthinkable. It had to be Abigail.

Emma had thought of staying at a friend's house instead of living at home, trying to protect herself by simply not being here, but then Christopher would be alone with Abigail. And besides, what would it do to her reputation to move out of her own house and into a friend's? Her plan was much smarter. She would try to get Christopher to see Abigail for what she really was, and in the meantime, she could work Mr. Pendlebury up to marriage. By the time Christopher finally understood—and perhaps they could prove Abigail was responsible, or at the very least that something was wrong with her—Emma would be engaged and her future would be settled. She could move out of this dreadful house without having to worry about Christopher. He would have Abigail put away, if she didn't go to jail, on the grounds of hysteria or something similar. It would not be difficult.

For the moment, she was becoming desperate for

Christopher to come to his senses. And now he'd called Abigail "kind". It was more than Emma could bear.

"Abigail is not *kind* at all," Emma spat, more harshly than intended. "Abigail is doing what's best for Abigail. That's what I'm trying to tell you. She's spending down the money so we won't have enough to be marriageable prospects. I won't have a satisfactory dowry and you won't have enough to attract a wife." She paused, allowing the idea to sink in and hopefully fall into place. "Then we'll be here forever. Like her."

Christopher's eyes unclouded. The doubt erased and clarity sparkled. *Thank goodness.* He nodded. "I will ask her. Nicely at first, of course. But if she refuses, that will be our answer."

"Exactly," Emma agreed.

*

Abigail didn't like it when people hid from her. It could be called paranoia, but it could also be called intelligence. If people weren't where you could see or hear them, they might be talking about you.

Abigail was aware of where everyone was in the house most of the time. She had quite good hearing, for a start, and she didn't daydream much, so when someone's footsteps were audible, she heard them no matter what she was doing or how engrossed in it she was.

In Christopher's room, there was no sound of the turning pages of a book. In Emma's room, there was no sound of her shifting in bed. When Abigail crept downstairs, neither of them was in the parlor, nor in the dining room. But as she was about to leave the dining room, she heard a sound like a voice. It could only be coming from the kitchen. The kitchen staff was no longer working this evening, so it wouldn't be them. There were only two people left who could be talking in there, a place where only servants ventured.

Abigail backed out of her slip-on bedroom shoes and placed her heel on the floor, rolling the rest of her foot down until her toes were grounded. She did this quietly but quickly. She had practice. Her heart raced at the thought of missing an important conversation she needed to know about.

Finally she reached the door and squatted carefully so her skirts didn't crush too loudly. She put her ear to the keyhole.

"...spending down the money—" it was Emma's voice, "so we don't have enough to be marriageable prospects. I won't have a satisfactory dowry and you won't have enough to attract a wife. Then we'll be here forever. Like her."

After all I've done for them both, how can she speak of me this way? Have I not warned her not to get involved where she doesn't need to be? Christopher will negate this.

"I will ask her," came Christopher's voice, and that was all she needed to hear. Abigail crept back to her shoes and quietly went back upstairs.

Obviously they were going to check the bank balance. Christopher could easily go to the bank and ask them about the balance and have a rough idea of whether it sounded reasonable, but he was giving her the benefit of the doubt. Knowing Christopher's gentle nature, he probably didn't want to go behind her back. She had to change the numbers, fast. What if he wanted to see the balance tonight?

Abigail reached her room and closed the door softly. If

she stayed there, she could either feign sleep if he knocked on the door, or if he opened the door, feign illness. She kept everything she didn't want others to see in her room, so the finances were there as well. Thank goodness for that. If they'd been in the study, Christopher could check them without her consent. Clearly neither of them could be trusted with things left in common areas.

Out of a drawer in her dresser, Abigail clawed at her nightgowns until she found the ledger and a blank one for when she ran out of room in this one. There were a lot of pages in it, pages with Father's handwriting. She went to her bed and reached under the mattress where she'd cut a hole in it and took out stationary paper. It should have been in the study or even the parlor, but she kept extra here too in case she ever needed to write a letter neither of her siblings should see. This was one of those cases. Only it wasn't a letter she needed to pen. It was her Father's handwriting, and she needed to practice quickly. She sat down at her writing desk and picked up her pen, dipping it into the inkwell. Frantically she wrote the first word in the ledger over and over again: damask wallpaper cleaning. Five times she tried with no improvement. She stopped and raised her head to the ceiling, closing her eyes.

Stop. Breathe. Calm down. Relax. You can do this, just concentrate.

She looked back down at the pen and paper. First, she studied her father's script carefully: how softly the "m" curved, the slant of the "l", how the first letter of each word was fancier than the others and the last always had an upward curve.

Picking up the pen, Abigail tried again to write the words "damask wallpaper" on the scrap stationery. Very slowly she copied. She wished the stationery was thin enough that she could place it on top of the ledger and see through the paper so she could trace the letters. The first try was shaky, but not as bad as before. Her script was too stiff in general. She needed to loosen it, make it a bit more flowery, not as thin. She tried again and got her "l" to tilt. Again, and the flounce at the end looked more natural. She must have tried it more than fifty times before she felt confident enough to work in the blank ledger.

Abigail wrote by the light of an oil lamp, and she realized its light might be visible under her door. She didn't want Christopher and Emma to know she was awake. She had to block the light at the door. Stuffing a blanket there would be easy to spot if anyone looked, plus she didn't have a black blanket to blend in with what the room would look like if it was dark.

Her dress. Her mourning dress was black. Abigail quickly changed into a nightdress and laid her dress down on the floor against the door, but didn't shove it underneath. She folded the dress in half to make sure it was tall enough to cover the whole gap and put it just touching the door so no fabric could slip underneath.

Abigail spent much of the night copying from one book into the other. How many hours, she couldn't say. She'd stopped the clock in her room long ago. She'd always hated the sound.

October 16, 1860

Abigail happened to be walking past the front door when she noticed Emma on her way out, hand on the knob.

"Where are you going?" Abigail asked.

The knob turned.

"Emma," Abigail said with a harsh edge, then softer, "where are you going?"

Emma turned slowly. She looked perfectly respectable in her dark blue visiting gown, of course, but Abigail still needed to know. It was her responsibility.

"I'm only going to visit with Mary," Emma said, her patience clearly thin. "I won't be long."

"One hour," Abigail said. She stared solidly into her sister's eyes, unblinking.

"Abigail, I'll be back when I'm ready to come home. No more than two hours. Mary and I always have so much to talk about and I hate to leave too soon for no—"

"Tea is at four o'clock, Emma, you know that." Her voice was unwavering.

"I can take tea there, Abigail, you know *that*. Stop trying to control everything in this house. How can I have a normal social life under your roof? Society will think me odd if I act like you."

A pause. Emma wasn't going to take that back. Her eyes were shy, but her stance was straight and solid.

Abigail took a clacking step forward. "So you think I'm odd." She stood rigidly straight.

Emma was uncertain how to respond to this. What would be the consequence of taking it back? Of not taking it back? She chose to say nothing, let God decide her fate.

"You know I've always had your best interest at the

forefront of everything I do, of all I've taught you. You know I have dedicated my life to you and Christopher." She crept forward slowly. "You know I've been here for everything, big and small, and I always will be. I do what is best—always." It was a heavy pause with unflinching eye contact, hard and unnatural. Abigail stopped her forward motion within inches of her sister's face. "As you know, Mary is nothing like her Biblical name. She is popular among men in the most unfortunate way possible. Visiting with her for extended periods of time will bring your reputation to her level. You should not be known as her cohort, you should be known only as her acquaintance, her nice, sweet, charitable acquaintance who has morals and respect for herself and her family. Without that reputation, any marriage you take will be riddled with the same moral problems you put on display simply in your choice of best friend. I don't want that for you." Pause. "Is that so odd?"

Emma swallowed so that her throat moved visibly and obviously. Her stare wavered. Perhaps she was being too harsh to Abigail and too lenient with her choice of friend. Or perhaps she should be allowed to make her own decision.

"How many friends have you, Abigail?" Emma asked.

Abigail finally looked uncertain.

"I asked how many friends you have. From my knowledge of your social life, the answer is none. And so you are qualified to recite rules and regulations and the like, but you are not, by way of real experience, able to advise me on modern matters and how life changes and wavers in its consequences. Mary is dealing with a broken engagement, and so I'm paying a call to help her work through that, a matter well known by the town, thoroughly talked about, and understood. I *am* her sweet, charitable acquaintance, Abigail, and I am acting not only as societal rules allow, but as a human being should. Any future husband would commend my compassion, and any man who doesn't is a man I don't want." It hung in the air that a man similar to Abigail in his line of thinking would be looked down upon—rejected—by Emma, and in that same air hung Emma's true opinion of Abigail.

Emma swung the door open. "I'll return when my visit is concluded." And she left. The closed door seemed shadowed, deeply shadowed. It seemed to grow darker by the moment. Mother would never have let Abigail get away with that. But Emma. Emma could get away with anything. Anything.

Abigail's breathing thickened. It was as if she couldn't take in enough air to satisfy her lungs. Her eyes were perfectly round buttons, dry. Fists bunched the fabric of her dress. Her jaw tweaked.

Throwing one foot out in a giant step in front of her, she screamed a startling howl, short and pained, frustrated and angry. The noise was piercing, bloodcurdling, filled every molecule of air around her. Her throat felt tight and her mouth pulled back in a baring of teeth only an animal could manage.

"Abigail," said Christopher from behind her, just a little more than a whisper. She turned smoothly on the heel of her shoe to find him halfway down the stairs mid stride. He looked confused and disdainful, one hand on the banister.

She drew one slower, heavier breath, her chest pushing out, pressing against her dress. She pointed toward the sitting room.

"Tea will be in exactly one hour," she said, her voice a

shaky low growl. "We have something to discuss."

*

"If you have to be in mourning," Mary said, "you couldn't look prettier."

"Thank you," Emma said, then sipped her tea. "Wearing black every day only makes it worse. It certainly doesn't help."

"It's easier for men. They wear a lot of black anyway." Mary put her teacup and saucer down and took up her plate with a scone. "How is Christopher?"

"He's fine," Emma said. "If you want to win him, just feed him well."

Mary raised her eyebrows. "Why do you say that?"

"Oh nothing." Emma sighed. "More importantly how are *you* feeling? Has there been a letter from him?"

Mary bit her lip. "No letter."

"I think the next time something like this happens, you should take my advice," Emma scolded gently. "Men don't like to be chased."

"I know, I should never have sent it," Mary said. "It was a terrible idea to beg him to rethink his decision."

"You should have let him go," Emma said.

"And what about yours?" Mary asked.

"I'll tell you all about him while we're in town," Emma said, smiling. She pointed conspiratorially at the door. Mary's parents were home, and you never knew when they might come in.

"I don't know if I can wait that long!" Mary said. "Let's go now."

"I haven't finished my tea yet," Emma said.

"We'll have more tea when we return," Mary said, picking up a large box from a chair against the wall.

"What is that?" Emma asked of the box.

"Oh, I want to go to the doll shop and ask if they have another doll like this one," Mary said, sitting down again. "I want to get the same one for my cousin. She'd just adore it." Mary took the lid off the box. Inside was a bisque doll with a brown dress. Emma's heart hitched and her head felt as if it had been hit hard. Air gushed out of her mouth and she couldn't take any more in.

"Emma?" She heard Mary's voice through a fog. The lid went back on the box. A small breath passed through Emma's throat, then another. Emma startled at something next to her on the couch. It was Mary.

"Emma, you look like you're going to faint," Mary said. "What's wrong?"

"I-I…" Emma scratched at the spot where her heart still beat so hard it almost hurt. "I don't know. All of a sudden… I don't know what came over me."

"Perhaps we'd better stay here," Mary said.

"Yes, let's not leave," Emma said. Mary put the box back where it came from. Emma's heart slowed down.

*

At four o'clock on the dot, Christopher came to the parlor and sat in his chair. The tea service had already been set out by the servants a little early, as Abigail had requested, so that it would be ready for him.

"Abigail—"

"I'll pour you some tea, Christopher," Abigail said as she poured it. "Would you like a piece of cake?"

"No," Christopher said plainly. "Abigail—"

"It's sponge cake and very well made. We are so lucky our cook—"

"Your actions are inexplicable," Christopher said,

198

overrunning her words.

Abigail rolled her lips inward and bit down.

"A lady doesn't scream like that at a door. At her sister!" Christopher exclaimed. Abigail had never seen her brother even close to irritated before. He didn't seem to like her mistreatment of Emma. But it wasn't mistreatment. If only he could understand that.

Softly, Abigail said, "You are right, Christopher. I apologize. It was far too extreme."

He held his hand out for his tea. That must have satisfied him to some degree. Now he needed to ask for the finances so she could prove she was not the monster he'd witnessed an hour earlier. She hoped he would ask. She was fidgety at his annoyance.

"I lost my head for a moment." She looked down at her tea. "It's just that Emma makes such a fool of herself with her choice of friends and the man with whom she keeps company."

"She was going to see Mary, so I can only assume you mean her," Christopher said. Abigail immediately wondered what conversation Emma and Christopher had without her in which Emma had told him her plans for the day. She hadn't told Abigail. "Well, what's wrong with Mary? What problem could you have with her?"

Abigail sighed audibly and said, "I don't have a problem with Mary. Mary can do whatever she pleases, but I feel she's influencing Emma. I only want what's best for her." Abigail put her tea down. "Don't you think Mr. Pendlebury is a little bit old for Emma?"

Christopher shook his head automatically but then stopped, considering. "What is it, something like seventeen years' difference? But it would be a good marriage for her.

He has substantial wealth."

"Yes, but wasn't he engaged to a young lady once and that engagement was broken? Wasn't it because he showed interest in another lady?" Abigail asked. If Christopher could come to his own conclusion with only some goading from Abigail, perhaps he would let her alone. Perhaps he would convince Emma to break the courtship.

"That might be true," Christopher said, "but it's not such a crime for a man of wealth like him. I wouldn't call it a quality of his, it's expected to some extent, but it's not a good thing for the ladies he's involved with either."

"I just think of Mary and what she's going through with her broken engagement..." Abigail didn't finish the sentence. She knew nothing more of Mary's situation than the little Emma had said before she left. She waited for Christopher to understand what she was implying and hoped he wouldn't ask any questions about Mary. She didn't want to lie. She wanted to insinuate.

"You worry the same will happen to Emma?" he asked.

"Mr. Pendlebury has already proven himself... Well, perhaps not of poor quality, like you said, but he's proven to have a roaming eye at the very least."

"I suppose if Emma were to marry him, his eye could still wander," Christopher said. "Quite true." He was lost in thought for a few moments. "I think I should speak with her about it. Can you pass me a piece of sponge cake?"

Abigail smiled. "Yes, of course." She picked up the plate and brought it over to him instead of reaching across the rug.

"I will be gentle," he said, "but she should see things objectively. We don't want her to get hurt."

"We don't want her to get hurt," Abigail repeated.

"Which reminds me, I've been meaning to ask you how our bank account is doing with you at the helm," he said nonchalantly. He seemed almost chummy. "Everything's going well?"

"Of course," Abigail said. "It's really very simple. I keep careful track of all our expenses and our income."

"Good," Christopher said. "I wouldn't mind a peek at it myself, if you don't mind. Perhaps I can learn more from you than Father would have taught me."

"I will bring it down now," Abigail said.

"No need to rush and bring it during tea," Christopher said.

"I don't want to forget," Abigail said. She went upstairs and got the new ledger from her bedroom. She was nervous, her hands a little sweaty. She hoped they didn't leave any sweat on the leather of the book. She went back downstairs and handed it to him with her finger holding it open to the most recently updated page.

"Here you are," she said and poured him more tea.

"Thank you, Abigail," Christopher said. "You know I'm not checking on your ability to keep this up to date, I just would like to know how our expenses have changed or stayed the same."

"Of course I know that," she said, smiling. Sitting down, Abigail placed her hands flat on her lap, waiting to see if it had worked. Christopher held the page with his forefinger and started at the front. He was probably looking at the expenses from Father's time of handling the book to compare the numbers. He slowly flipped through some pages, taking his time. He looked up at her.

"You don't have to wait for my reaction, you can work on your embroidery or read a book," he said.

"Oh yes, I just thought if you had any questions. I want to make sure you think I've done a good job," she said, nerves coming into her voice. It probably came across as nervousness over Christopher's opinion. She hoped that was how it came across.

He smiled and continued reading.

Abigail bit her lip and picked up *The Black Tulip*, the only book she'd had an interest in since Conrad had stopped their courtship. She read nothing. Just listened for sounds of approval or disappointment. She heard nothing.

"This all looks quite good, Abigail, I'm impressed," Christopher said. "There's just one thing."

"Yes?" she asked. Her heart felt like it was twisting inside her chest.

He continued to look down and put his finger on the spot. "Come here."

She stood and walked over to him.

"What is this? Does this say 'duplicate key'?" Christopher asked.

Abigail swallowed. She had to say this correctly and convincingly. "That's right, it does."

"What duplicate key?" Christopher asked.

"Well…it's not really my business," she said. When Christopher looked up at her, she made sure to look away. "I'd rather not tell you."

"What is it? Why would a key need to be kept a secret?" he asked.

"Emma had it made," Abigail said, and left the false fact hanging on the edge of its dangerous precipice.

"Did she lose hers?" Christopher asked.

"No, she said it was for Mary, in case Mary wanted to come over sometime," Abigail said.

"Mary? Mary can knock, can't she?" Christopher said.

"I know. I asked her many times why Mary needed a key to our house, but I could never get a satisfactory answer from her. I just hope..."

"You hope what?"

Abigail waited a moment, trying to look worried.

"I hope it really was for Mary," she said in a hushed tone.

Christopher frowned up at her and turned his face away a little. Abigail couldn't tell whether he looked uncertain or unhappy with this inference. He said nothing and handed the book back to her, now in a foul mood. She took it and went back up to her room to return it to its place beneath her nightdresses before Emma returned.

When she sat back down in the sitting room, Christopher said, "If you ever see Pendlebury come here again, let me know. I'd like to speak to him."

October 25, 1860

Abigail stared at the lock intently. The doorknob that had had no choice but to lock her in her room so many times was solid metal with thin, gentle curling flourishes standing off it. She had never really looked at it closely before. But the design stood off far. Quite far. She imagined Mother's hand reaching down to open the door in such an angry mood that she would grab hold of the handle hard and burn the whole design onto her palm. She would have deserved that for all the times Abigail was trapped behind it.

She ran one finger down the front of the doorknob, making sure to feel every protrusion very well. Carefully maneuvering her dress to kneel, she took a piece of paper and a small pencil out of the side slit pocket of her dress. With the piece of paper pressed against the cold metal knob, she ran her pencil gently over the paper and took down the impression of the design. She watched it dirty the clean ivory surface and pressed harder. She knew the pencil would tear a hole if she kept increasing the pressure, so she forced herself to stop. One more time she felt the design with her finger, following one of the slim vine-like curves in its swirl that seemed to go on and on forever. She would keep this tracing to remind her of what no longer held her back.

Abigail stood abruptly, went straight downstairs, and left the house. She would be sure to be back before supper. No one would know the difference.

*

There was a knock on the front door and Emma stood in the parlor, waiting. Ashdon answered it with her usual greeting and allowed the man inside. While he took off his hat and gloves, Ashdon went into the parlor and startled slightly when she saw Emma standing so close to the doorway.

"Mr. Pendlebury is here to see you, miss," she said.

"Thank you, I'll come out to meet him. I'll be home late, so don't bolt the door," Emma said.

The maid smiled, said "Of course, miss," and left the room.

"Miss Whitestone will be here in a moment, sir," Ashdon said to Mr. Pendlebury.

As soon as the maid passed the parlor on her way to the back of the house, Emma came out to meet him.

"My, you look lovely tonight, Emma," Mr. Pendlebury said. His evening clothes were impeccable as usual. Emma couldn't wear anything colorful since the house was still in mourning, and she couldn't dance either, but she could attend and still look attractive. She didn't want to be shown up by the lovely dresses of all the other ladies, although she knew there wasn't much she could do and still be found socially respectable. She complemented her dress with only a simple black bead necklace, the beads beautifully faceted; mourning jewelry made of Mother's hair had never appealed to her or Abigail, so none had been made. And she couldn't honestly say she missed Mother, so it would have been like wearing a lie. Her dress was black because it was expected, and for no other reason.

"Thank you very much, Bennett. Will we go now or sit for a while first?" she asked politely.

"Let's go now, my dear," he said, motioning toward the door.

"Ah, Mr. Pendlebury," Christopher said from the stairs

as he came down. "How good to see you. I believe I've met you only once before."

"Mr. Whitestone, it's good to see you as well. I'm very sorry to hear of your mother's death," he said, holding his hand out to shake.

"Thank you," Christopher said, taking the outstretched hand. "Before you go, I'd like a word."

"Christopher, we were just leaving. Perhaps next time?" Emma said. She formed it as a question but meant it as a statement. She wanted to get out of the house.

"No, this time, Emma," he said, smiling. "Why don't you work on your embroidery upstairs for now."

Emma knew there was nothing she could say to this; she just had to accept it. "Tell me when you've finished," she said.

"She's really quite good at embroidery," Christopher said as Emma left the room.

Why did he suddenly want to speak to Mr. Pendlebury? This was unlike Christopher. Usually he was so relaxed. He'd never asked after a suitor of hers before, and she'd had a few. He was a tactful man, though, so she couldn't be too skeptical. She would wait upstairs as he asked.

*

There was a knock on Emma's door, but it was too soon to be Christopher telling her his chat with Mr. Pendlebury was over. She opened the door to find Abigail standing with her hands clasped in front of her.

"Don't you look lovely, Emma," she said. "Are you going out tonight?"

"Yes," Emma said, surprised to receive a compliment from Abigail. This was the first time ever. "Christopher is downstairs talking to Mr. Pendlebury now. We will be leaving after they finish."

"Oh good, that gives me enough time to show you something," Abigail said and waved at Emma to follow her.

They went across the hall to the governess's old room. It was only used for sparc bits and bobs now, and Emma couldn't remember the last time she had gone inside. Abigail walked in first and headed straight for the old bed, keeping her back to Emma and picking something up.

"Wait just a moment," Abigail said. "I want it to be perfect… There!" She whirled around to face Emma. She held in front of her a light green dress Emma had never seen before.

"What's this, Abigail?" Emma asked.

"It's Mother's old wedding dress!" Abigail exclaimed. Emma hadn't heard her sound excited before. It was odd and forced. "I thought you might want it for your wedding. I assume Mr. Pendlebury will ask you soon."

Emma was stunned into silence. "I didn't think you cared for Mr. Pendlebury."

"I didn't do this for him, I did it for you," Abigail said.

Emma was doubtful but couldn't think of a reason why Abigail would do this if it wasn't out of what little compassion she might have inside her. "That's very nice of you, Abigail. It does look like it might fit me, too."

"Well that's because I already had it tailored for you," Abigail said. She was smiling. Sort of a Cheshire cat smile.

"You did?" Emma asked. "Abigail, that's such a kind thing to do! What a nice surprise." Emma took it from Abigail and held it up against herself.

"I just wish it was a more fashionable color," Abigail said.

"Will you come with me to buy the rest of the outfit?

Shoes?" Emma asked. She had already lost control of her heart and was smiling herself now.

"Oh yes, of course I will," Abigail said. "Won't it be lovely?"

Emma looked up at Abigail and noticed something different about her dress.

"Is that new?" Emma asked.

"Oh no, I wouldn't spend that kind of money on myself. I only spend money on you and Christopher," Abigail said purposefully. Emma's mind immediately flitted to her conversation in the kitchen with Christopher, but the memory dissipated quickly. "This dress is only new to me. It was Mother's."

Emma didn't understand. "Mother's?"

"Yes. I thought it would be wasteful to give her dresses away or sell them. So I had them fitted to me," Abigail said, spinning around to show all angles of the dress.

"But... But you and Mother..." Emma started but was afraid her words would sound unkind.

"Yes?" Abigail waited. It was at that moment Emma knew that Abigail wanted her to say, "But Mother abused you so," or "But you hated Mother," as an excuse. An excuse for what, Emma hadn't figured out. She only knew she had to be careful.

"You and Mother were quite different sizes," Emma finished very carefully. "Oh, but you already said you had them fitted for you. Of course. You're much slimmer than she was."

Abigail looked disappointed. Emma had been right.

"I am," Abigail said. "Quite different from Mother."

That was where she was wrong, and Emma wondered what other trap she had just fallen into in accepting

Mother's wedding gown. She knew already that this one, whatever it was, would be particularly bad.

*

"Please sit down, Mr. Pendlebury," Christopher said, holding his hand out to his usual chair. "This is my favorite seat, so please take it."

"Good of you, Mr. Whitestone, thank you," Mr. Pendlebury said, sitting slowly, a dead giveaway of their age difference.

Ashdon entered and slowed as she saw Emma was no longer there.

"Shall I bring you—" she began, but Christopher interrupted

"There is no need, Ashdon," he said. "Mr. Pendlebury won't be here long." Christopher turned back to his guest and asked flatly, "How are you these days, Mr. Pendlebury?"

"Quite well, thank you," Mr. Pendlebury said. "And yourself?"

"Not bad. The funeral was a month ago, but I think we're managing."

"Yes, my deepest condolences for the loss of your mother," he said. "It was a beautiful affair."

"It was," Christopher said. "But I didn't see you in attendance."

"I wasn't sent an invitation," Mr. Pendlebury said.

"Ashdon says one was delivered to you," Christopher said, "without my approval, of course."

"Well—"

"How many times have you visited or taken my sister out?" Christopher asked.

"At least five times, perhaps more," Mr. Pendlebury

said, sounding uncertain of this line of questioning. His answer sounded too off-the-cuff for Christopher's taste. "We haven't been able to see each other steadily. I have quite a full social calendar, you know."

"But you *think* five times," Christopher said.

Mr. Pendlebury nodded. "Yes, approximately."

"And you call my sister by her first name already?" Christopher said. He relaxed into Abigail's chair but kept his hands clasped on his lap and his back straight. He had chosen that chair for a reason: its height.

"Miss Whitestone has recently agreed to deepen our acquaintance," Mr. Pendlebury said.

"Without approval from me," Christopher said, "and as far as I know, without approval from our father. Correct me if I'm wrong, of course."

Mr. Pendlebury shifted his legs uncomfortably. "With respect, your father...disappeared before I could ask."

"Ah, I see," Christopher said. "So you've asked Emma after only five times in her company, and only since my father's disappearance and our mother's death, during our time of mourning."

Mr. Pendlebury froze. There was nothing he could say except the truth, and that was a bad idea. His silence confirmed his breach of manners.

"I also understand you've broken an engagement in the past," Christopher said. "A relationship with another *young* lady?" Mr. Pendlebury had to be made to understand that Christopher was no fool about the older man's interests.

"That is correct, Mr. Whitestone, but she did accept it. I didn't break ties in a painful way, you see, I was quite gentle," Mr. Pendlebury tried to explain.

"Not a comfort, sir," Christopher said. He slid forward

in his chair. "I would like to ask you something from one gentleman to another, Mr. Pendlebury." His eyes didn't falter from Mr. Pendlebury's. He enunciated carefully, "If you are not entirely sure at this point whether you will marry my sister, I must ask you to use your experienced judgment to decide whether you should continue to pursue her. Because if you do not relent and you should break an engagement to her," he still hadn't blinked, "we will not make it so easy for your reputation to remain unblemished." Christopher pursed his lips. "Do you understand me well, Mr. Pendlebury?"

Mr. Pendlebury examined the younger man's face. "Perfectly."

Christopher stood. "Then we are done here."

*

Emma came downstairs when she heard the front door close.

When she reached the parlor and saw only Christopher sitting pensively, she stopped dead in the doorway.

"Where's Mr. Pendlebury?" she asked, not hiding her worry.

Christopher tapped his fingers on his lap and didn't look at her. "He has gone."

"But why?" she asked, walking farther into the room to face him.

He stood up. "Why?" he said, a tinge of anger in his voice. "Bennett, as you so familiarly called him, was given a choice, and he decided he wasn't serious about you. I'm thoroughly disappointed in your choice of suitors, Emma, knowing what kind of a man he is before you became this deeply involved. He doesn't love you and he wasn't planning to. I certainly hope your morals are still intact."

His face was red, a color foreign to it.

Emma said nothing while her head throbbed with the loss of not just love but escape.

"I suppose all I can do is hope," he said, quieter now. But something worse was in his voice. Disgust. Which was exactly what he should have felt toward Abigail. But now, he felt it for her.

*

When Emma reached the top of the steps on her way back to her room, Abigail was waiting in the hall.

"Aren't you going out with Mr. Pendlebury tonight?" she asked.

Emma felt an overwhelming surge of contempt looking at Abigail in Mother's dress.

"Mr. Pendlebury left, actually," Emma said, working hard to tame her feelings.

"Why?" Abigail asked.

Emma couldn't bring herself to answer. She tried to walk past Abigail, but Abigail wouldn't let her.

"Will he come by tomorrow instead?" she asked.

"He won't be visiting anymore, Abigail," Emma said sharply.

As wide as Abigail's eyes became, they couldn't truly cover themselves with a mask of shock.

"I can't imagine!" Abigail said. "How could this have happened?"

"I don't know," Emma lied. "I'm going to bed."

"Oh, but there will be plenty of other men, younger than him and nicer, I'm sure," Abigail said, putting her hand on Emma's shoulder. This was far from the affection Emma had shown Abigail when Mr. Scott had broken off their courtship, but it was still more than expected from

Abigail. "Come downstairs and we'll drink chocolate. I'll have some too."

Emma didn't know what to make of this, but either Abigail was using this as an opportunity to become closer to Emma or Abigail had had some part in it in the first place. Those were the only two conclusions Emma could come to. But if she said no, she feared Abigail would be upset, and Emma couldn't deal with that now too.

"Thank you, Abigail," Emma said, and they walked down to the kitchen together, where they spent a silent half hour stirring and sipping their drinks. *So odd*, Emma thought, *to go through all this trouble just to sit in silence. So very odd.*

November 13, 1860

The workman unscrewed the lock from Emma's door, the screw squeaking as he did so. She had stopped short in the hallway as soon as she saw him squatting in front of her door. He glanced up at her, then took a longer look. Surprised, he stood up.

"Afternoon, miss. I'm just replacin' the doorknobs 'n' locks." He smiled, dipped his head a little, and returned to work. A new lock was being put on Emma's door now. A new lock she hadn't been told about.

"May I ask who called you to do this?" Emma asked politely, softly.

The workman stood again. "Miss Whitestone, miss. She called Locke and Keye, the shop where I work, a few weeks ago 'n' picked out the locks 'n' keys herself. The shop owner had the doorknobs made special for her, that's why it took so long." He sounded apologetic for a wrong he hadn't committed. "I'll just return to my work, if ya don't mind. I have ta have this job finished today. Miss Whitestone's orders." He dipped his head again and squatted back down.

Emma squinted for lack of an idea of what to do first: ask Abigail what was going on or ask Christopher if he knew anything about this. If she asked Abigail, she might find out...might. But Christopher would most likely know nothing more than Emma did. In fact, he might even be out. Yes...yes, he had mentioned calling on a friend of his today around this time. How carefully planned this was. Just so carefully planned.

Abigail *clunk*ed around the corner, her skirts giving away that she had stopped quite short when she'd spotted

Emma.

"Why Emma, what are you doing home so soon? I thought you were going for a walk with Mary. You've really ruined my surprise."

"Surprise? That the locks are being changed? Why would that be a *nice* surprise, Abigail?" Emma had too much of an edge to her voice.

"Well, I thought the doorknobs could use some... beautifying. Don't you think they look so much nicer?"

Emma paused, evaluating her older sister. She was sure her eyes showed the calculations going on inside her head. "It's just that you could certainly have changed the doorknobs to be more fashionable, but you could have requested the same locks and keys be kept." Her voice was flat, monotone. It was a tone that refuted Abigail's story.

Abigail's shoulders did a quick back and forth as she squared herself against Emma. Somehow she always looked so imposing when she did that. She looked like an old dead oak tree that couldn't be moved even in the fiercest wind. Emma knew what this meant.

"The locks are being changed for our protection. I believe a key has gotten into the hands of a man who should never have had a key in the first place." This was not true. "I've tried to save your honor by making this a happy occasion, but you've refused to allow that. Your poor reputation is proving itself dangerous, Emma. No one will have the keys to this house or any of its rooms except me from this day forward. And when Christopher asks why his keys no longer work, you may choose which to tell him: my happier version or the truth."

Abigail's heavy skirts swished as she passed her sister aggressively in the hall, her stare boring into the side of

Emma's head. From behind Emma, the *clunk*ing stopped. "And if you are still courting such a lecherous man without telling us, he will not be permitted to sit in this house. You will not embarrass this family with your poor judgement." The stairs pounded beneath Abigail's shoes as she descended.

Emma stared at the workman in the hall. He was being so gracious, pretending not to have heard a word. His eyes were fixed on the lock. He had finished screwing the new doorknob and plate in halfway through Abigail's speech, but he feigned continuing his task to avoid interrupting the explosion of information that should never have met his ears. Abigail had done that on purpose. Abigail was trying to ruin her reputation in a backdoor manner. And yet…had she found out that she still met with Mr. Pendlebury? Perhaps other ladies around town talked behind her back of their relationship? Perhaps her own friends?

When Emma realized the workman was standing in front of her, she also realized she had been staring at the wallpaper, running her finger over the curved edges of the black velvet design. He was alarmingly close now.

He glanced behind her before saying, "Just wonderin', miss, it's just that I've never seen a broke doll collection like Miss Whitestone's before. I have some broke dolls myself. D'you know anyone who could tell me their price? Or per'aps Miss Whitestone… It's just I thought I could make some extra money off what my daughter's broke."

She stared at him with wide eyes. "Broken…dolls, did you say?"

"Yeah." He turned around and pointed to their parents' old room. "When I was changin' that room's lock, I couldn't keep from seein' through the hole when the knob was off—all those damaged dolls in there. 'N' I thought that'd be a good way ta bring in some money. I don't know another reason anybody would keep those kindsa things."

Emma nodded slowly. "I don't think my sister would mind if you asked her yourself," she said carefully,

"Thank you, miss, I'll be sure ta ask her."

As he moved his box of equipment to another door, she stood stock still where she was. She would visit the workman in the next few days and find out what Abigail had said about the dolls. What an odd thing to collect in their parents' room, a room she and her brother were not allowed to go into. Come to think of it, why couldn't she enter their parents' room? Perhaps she would persuade Christopher to question Abigail on that matter without actually asking him. His natural curiosity would get the better of him.

She would force the issue at dinner.

*

Supper was quail that night. Quail was a favorite of Christopher's, and Abigail had probably figured that he'd appreciate it, making the lock changes also seem like a positive thing, like one big happy day and evening. Emma knew her sister as well as one could know Abigail. Somehow it always seemed that Abigail was doing what was best for Emma, but at the same time, it was like a jigsaw puzzle piece that looks like it should fit exactly in one spot except for the small jagged edge that doesn't quite fit the soft edges of its intended place. The piece about which everyone said, "I can't even imagine where this goes" until the very end.

"You might notice some changes around here," Abigail said almost cheerily. "Some beautifying?"

Christopher looked up from his knife working into the meat of the quail on his plate. "I hadn't noticed anything," he said, putting a piece in his mouth and chewing hungrily.

"You will when you go to bed this evening," she said, making it sound tempting. She smiled a small half circle, keeping her eyes on his while her face was turned mostly to her plate.

"You'll notice you can't get in," Emma said. She refused to look at Abigail, whose eyes she could feel creating holes in her temple. "Or is Christopher well behaved enough in your eyes to receive his own keys, Abigail?"

"Keys?" Christopher asked. Emma was sure he wouldn't notice if Abigail threw the bread knife at her, so she knew he certainly wouldn't notice the daggers being thrown from Abigail's eyes. There would be a price to pay for all this, she was sure. But this was too important to back down from. It was her access to her own home. What well-intentioned family member would take that away from another?

"Yes," Abigail began, clearly searching for what words she should say. Searching carefully. Emma felt herself being reevaluated. "Emma has quite spoiled the surprise, of course, but I've had all the locks and doorknobs and keys replaced throughout the house. You'll be happy when you see yours, Christopher. It represents you well." Abigail's eyes still hadn't left Emma, and Emma still hadn't returned the glare.

"How did you make that decision?" Christopher asked. "Wasn't it very expensive? Shouldn't you have consulted us?" Christopher may have been ignorant of obvious wordless parries, but he wasn't stupid. As the only male of the family left, his opinion was the most important, and he knew it.

"You remember how the old knobs squeaked so awfully when they were turned, and those rusted old keys. If you're both to have suitors calling, we can't look shabby," Abigail said, emphasizing the last two words. "Little details make all the difference when one knows what to look for, don't they, Emma?"

Why was she saying that?

"Of course, Abigail," Emma said, sounding more subservient than she meant to, so she added, "Who of good breeding doesn't know that." Her voice was monotone and stronger this time.

"It's also very important," continued Abigail, "to ensure the correct impression is always given, even to those whom we think are of no consequence. In fact, especially to those." A pause. "Family first."

Christopher was looking at Abigail, concerned. "Family first always, Abigail, none of us have ever questioned that." His face broke into a warm smile. "Is something on your mind?"

He must have known something was wrong too.

Something *was* wrong that was beyond Emma's comprehension. What was it? It was distinctly out of reach.

"It's just... Emma, you could have asked me yourself about the dolls."

Emma was taken aback. Her head flung to face her sister, her eyes sharp. "What?"

"The man who came to put in the new locks. He said you didn't seem to know about them, the ones in Mother and Father's room. He asked you a question and you didn't know they were even there. You could have asked me."

Abigail's hand reached out and took Emma's. There was no roughness to it, but it seemed there should have been. Honeyed though the conversation was, Emma still felt something was just beyond her understanding. "I'm surprised you don't remember them. They were yours when you were young. You used to leave dolls in my room for me to find, like gifts."

The grandfather clock's chime tolled loudly, sounding as if its tone meant something. *Dong.*

"You even put one in my bed once, remember?"

Dong. Insistent.

Emma did remember a doll. One that spilled dirt all over.

Dong.

She remembered being scared half to death by it.

Dong.

She remembered feeling all the warmth drain out of her body at its sight.

Dong.

There had been screaming. More than one voice.

Dong.

Abigail was watching Emma remember. Abigail's thumbnail dug lightly into Emma's palm, out of Christopher's sight.

Dong.

Emma couldn't put anything more to the memory than that fear. That must have been what triggered her to nearly faint at Mary's. "I remember," she said shakily.

Dong.

"You can see those dolls any time you'd like," Abigail said, taking her hand back. Emma withdrew hers as well. When she put her hands in her lap, she noticed her skin was prickled with goose bumps.

She wanted nothing to do with the dolls. She hoped she never saw one again.

*

"Abigail," came Christopher's voice from the stairs. He had followed her up after the dinner dishes were removed and she'd left the table instantly.

"Yes?" She turned halfway in the hallway.

"I appreciate that you had new locks put in, but I can't help but wonder… Why didn't you consult me first? We agreed to talk about major expenses before—"

"It wouldn't have been a surprise then, would it?" Abigail said, sounding short. She was losing patience with all this.

"No, it wouldn't. But I've been looking at the locks and doorknobs. All custom made? This must have cost a fortune. It wasn't necessary to get custom work done. Even the most attractive standard locks and keys and doorknobs would have been a better use of our money."

"I thought it would be special," Abigail said, lowering her voice.

"Nobody looks that closely," Christopher said, unmoved. "And Emma says you're keeping all the keys? Is that right? There can be no explanation for that, Abigail. I don't understand you. We are supposed to be completely open with each other, all of us."

"Then why didn't Emma ask me about the dolls in our parents' room?" It was said in a challenging way.

"It wasn't her question, it was the workman's question. So she referred him to you. She couldn't have handled it any other way."

Abigail squared her shoulders at him, her heel dragging

along the floor in a rounded sound that came across as threatening. Her eyes were open wide and almost crossed, they were so sharply focused on him. "Of course she couldn't have," she said softly. Christopher almost couldn't hear her. "Emma could never do anything wrong, could she?" Her head cocked slowly, smoothly, until it reached a 45 degree angle. "A workman asks Emma why there are broken dolls in our parents' room and she's not the least bit curious why they're there or whose they were? What would you call that, Christopher? Perhaps she remembers how she treated me when we were children. How she tortured me and teased me with those frightening dolls, and she's chosen to pretend she doesn't remember them at all, to erase part of our history together, to make her more perfect.

"Well, I remember. I remember all the times Mother took things away from me to give to Emma, all the times Emma gloated, she stole Mother's affection right in front of me, right *from* me, but all I do is take care of her. All I do is try to guide her and love her and warn her of mistakes she could make so she can have a clean and glowing reputation. And then to a *workman* of all people, someone who will talk to everyone in this town, she says she doesn't know anything about dolls in our own parents' room, like a secret had been kept from her all this time. It's disgraceful. All of it."

Abigail found herself bent over at the waist, spewing words at Christopher in a way she hadn't quite meant to, but she also didn't regret it. She had wanted to say every word of it, but she hadn't meant to sound angry. She'd meant to sound hurt, like a baby in need of protection from her evil sister. She needed Christopher to come to her defense instead of Emma's...permanently.

"Abigail, I—" Christopher started. He shook his head. "I don't know anything about those dolls either. Neither Emma nor I have seen that room. I would have said the same thing, not to embarrass you, but because it's the truth." He looked concerned. This was not the reaction Abigail had predicted. "She couldn't exactly lie to him, could she? Stumble over words and say, 'Oh, yes, they're my dead parents' and they're worth...' Something? Nothing? What was she to say?"

He raised his hands in a questioning gesture and dropped them loudly at his sides so they clapped against his pants. Then he put them away in his pockets. "If you have issues with Emma from when you were children, either work them out or forgive her when you pray. Involving a... a *workman* as a way to say this house's reputation is her fault—your entire relationship is her fault—well, that's not the way sisters should treat each other. It's not the Christian way. I think you know that." He paused and pulled his lips into his mouth. He looked completely secure in what he was saying. Like a father. Just like Father. "I'll expect my key tomorrow. I'm going to bed." He walked past her, hands still in pockets, his shoes barely making a sound other than the creaking of the wood. His soles sounded soft against the floor.

Abigail stood in the spot where he'd left her. She shook her head, staring at nothing in particular. She slowly raised her eyes and looked at the wallpaper next to her. Sometimes it seemed that the black design stood so far off the white paper, like a maze of bushes standing off the earth. She traced her sharp nail around the outside of a curve, sinking it deep into the fabric. She wondered if she could cut the design out with just her fingernail. She ran it across one spot over and over, and after a while—how long, she didn't know—the fabric split in one small area. She forced her fingernail underneath the wallpaper to widen the gap. A small hole in a dark place. Yes.

Abigail entered the Locke and Keye shop early in the morning when she knew nobody would be there. It was a wide open space with doorknobs, key samples, and locks lining the walls, but a spartan floor. She walked slowly to the front desk.

Clunk, clunk.

The clerk turned to face her, a young man she hadn't seen before.

"Good morning, madam. How can I help?" He wore a white, well-worn apron with stains that looked like creases.

"Good morning. I was hoping you could help me with some keys I just received from your shop. They were custom made, but I've now realized I need duplicates of each one." Abigail put her hand on the desk between them, gloved and refined. "I don't need the same ornate versions, just plain ones that fit the locks."

"On what account will this be placed, madam?" the clerk asked.

"Whitestone. And…I can pay you now. It's nothing you need to put on the account." Abigail reached her hand into her beaded bag and pulled out a small coin purse that she slid across the desk. "I'm sure this can push me to the front of your waiting list. When is the soonest you can finish the duplicates?"

"You can pick them up this afternoon, madam, one o'clock at the latest."

*

Abigail returned home at two o'clock with more than just plain duplicate keys that she would keep. The original keys that she would now give to Emma and Christopher were beautiful works of art. The bow of Christopher's key to his room had an ornate heart, unfilled in the center, with swirls of silver around it. Abigail's had a sweet flower shape with lovely twists and curves. But Emma's had no symbol on it. Just curls of metal, attractive, but not specific to her likes or Abigail's feelings for her. Or perhaps it was.

The front door key for each of them—thank goodness she'd thought far ahead enough to have three originals made for just this situation—had what ended up being a pretentious-looking abstract crown, a sort of inside joke among them all about the Whitestones making their way even further up the social ladder. They had no real jokes among them, but this could serve as one.

Abigail put the keys inside two black satin bags, one with Christopher's room key and house key, and one with Emma's room key and house key. To Christopher's, she added a solid gold pocket watch engraved with his initials, then tied it closed tightly. To Emma's, she added a pearl bracelet with an amethyst clasp and tied the bag closed with purple ribbon.

It was the guilt that made her include these gifts. They would never know about the copies, but Abigail had to have assurance that she could get into their rooms when she needed to. She didn't know when that would be, but they did tend to talk behind her back, and where there was that habit, there were often secrets. Secrets she could perhaps find in their diaries, letters... Anyway, she had the duplicate keys as a private promise that she could never be taken by surprise by either of them. And that was the greatest comfort she had ever felt.

*

Emma stood outside her room, inspecting her new key

in her hand. She hadn't seen Christopher's yet, but the house key... She took out the house key and put the two keys side by side in her hand. How intricate the one was compared to the other. Emma's had looked attractive until she'd seen the beautiful house key with something that looked like a crown—she wasn't sure why it would be a crown, though, so perhaps she was mistaken—and its lace-like metalwork.

Sighing, Emma used the key to open the door to her room and closed it behind her. She sat down on the bed and tried to relax her body, which had been increasingly tense since dinner, when Christopher found out about the new keys. She looked out her window. It was a beautiful evening with bright, clear stars. Perhaps she would leave the window open tonight.

Her eyes drifted aimlessly across her room, and she found herself staring at her dresser, her eyes unfocused at first. Something seemed odd to her. Nothing obvious was wrong, just... She couldn't put her finger on it.

Yes she could.

She stood up, took her oil lamp over to her dresser, and immediately realized that her clock was askew. Well, it was, wasn't it? Now she wasn't so sure, but she'd always been very exact about the way she kept her room. It was probably the most meticulous room in the house, although she'd never seen Abigail's room in all her life. It struck Emma how odd it was for her not to have seen her own sister's room all these years. And yet she felt no desire to. In fact, she felt a distinct deadening of her senses when she thought of going into that room.

Ah, there it was, now she saw it. On the dresser, a very light covering of dust stopped abruptly in a straight line where the clock should have sat. It was only off by a little bit, but she had always kept it facing her bed so she could see it when she first woke up. Now it was facing a little too far the other way. If there had been a slightly thicker covering of dust, the kind that could accrue if the surface hadn't been dusted during the day, she would have just assumed the chambermaid had somehow forgotten to dust this surface. She would have simply adjusted the angle of the clock herself and thought nothing of it. But the chambermaid clearly *had* dusted this surface; there was only a very thin veil of dust. Stranger still, her door had been locked—she'd just unlocked it herself—so nobody should have been in here but the chambermaid. And only Abigail had the key to let the chambermaid in.

Emma left her room and was poised to knock on Abigail's door, but she paused. What would Emma say? *Did you go into my locked room with the key I had with me and move things around?*

Still in front of Abigail's door, Emma looked down the hall in each direction before stooping, lifting the cover on the keyhole, and peeking in. She couldn't make out much —the bright stars shining softly from the window directly across from the door was not enough to see any amount of detail in the room. But that was more than she knew about her sister's room before—Abigail kept her drapes open. Emma had always imagined them closed at all times, blocking any hint of light.

Emma stood up, realizing she had no idea what she was looking for. She went back to her room. She must have somehow bumped the clock that morning, regardless of the fact that she knew that didn't happen. The alternatives were too unthinkable.

*

Abigail climbed the stairs with a book in her hand, holding her finger on the last page she had read. She'd found a good quote tonight that she didn't want to lose. She'd sew it onto an embroidered bookmark soon.

As she approached her door and reached her hand toward the knob, she noticed the ornate cover over the keyhole was slightly open. She dropped her hand. Had someone been trying to look into her room?

Emma's door was slightly ajar. Christopher was downstairs.

There was one way to find out.

Abigail had been relatively quiet coming upstairs. Perhaps…

It sounded like Emma was walking back and forth in her room. Perhaps pacing.

Abigail walked in place, making her footsteps sound softer, then louder, as if she were just now walking to her room. When she stopped, Abigail could hear nothing; Emma's pacing had also stopped. Abigail opened her own door, didn't go inside, and shut it. Emma continued moving about.

It *must* have been her peeping. But why? Abigail had been so careful in Emma's room. She couldn't have found out Abigail had been in there.

Unless…

Unless Emma knew Abigail was the one who had helped eliminate Pendlebury from her life. Had Christopher and Emma been talking again? Talking behind Abigail's back? Abigail knocked on Emma's door and heard her gasp, startled.

When Emma opened her door wider, she said, "Hello,"

with wide eyes and a too-big smile, her voice breathy.

Abigail smiled, but it didn't reach the corners of her mouth. It was more of a tightening of the lips. "I just wanted you to know that I heard someone in your room earlier," Abigail said. Silence. "It was the chambermaid. I must have forgotten to lock your door when she finished cleaning. I hope you haven't found anything missing."

A pause as Emma looked into each of Abigail's eyes. What was she looking for? "Nothing missing," Emma said stiffly.

"She's been let go," Abigail said. "I insisted."

"Oh," Emma said.

"Well shouldn't you thank me for catching her before she took something?" Abigail said. Abigail couldn't leave until she knew Emma trusted her, until she was convinced Emma believed her.

"Of course," Emma said, but she didn't thank her.

"And what about the bracelet?" Abigail pursued harder than she meant to. "You must have discovered it with your key."

"It's very lovely, Abigail." Still no thank you.

"Put it on," Abigail said, her voice flat.

"Excuse me?" Emma said, a glimmer of fear in her eyes. It must have been Abigail's tone. She felt her heart beat faster.

"I gave you something pretty, Emma," Abigail said, "and I'm the only one who has ever done that. That should mean something to you, shouldn't it?"

Emma opened her mouth but nothing came out. Nothing but a small squeak from the back of her throat.

"Unless someone else has given you pretty things too," Abigail said, raising her head to look down at Emma. "Are you still seeing him?"

Emma stepped backwards into her room and softly, quietly closed the door. It was the gentleness of the rejection that pushed Abigail one step too far.

January 12, 1861

Abigail had once read that memories from a person's extreme youth settled in the brain as feelings you couldn't quite place in your adult life. Where they had come from, you didn't always know. But often, if they were based in an event that induced fear, they resulted in phobias later in life.

The fear of dolls was a phobia.

Abigail had no phobias.

Abigail had been shown all the things to be scared of when she was young, outright.

Abigail had survived. She had not only survived—she had learned.

And no one could scare her anymore.

Emma went down the hallway heading to her room holding a book of poetry she'd been enjoying in the sitting room downstairs. As she approached her room, she noticed the door was open. Not wide open, but she knew she hadn't left it open at all.

She pushed the door the rest of the way open slowly, putting one foot across the threshold, looking around, and then entering fully and closing the door behind her. Now she noticed her closet door was ajar just a little bit. Funny. She certainly hadn't left that open either. But she was the only one with a key to her room, so... The closet door inexplicably made her nervous. She felt sweat form on her palms and wiped them on a handkerchief that was on her dresser. She stepped slowly toward the closet door, her anxiety rising. Her feelings made no sense to her, but she listened to them anyway and remained cautious.

Emma paused before the closet door and peered inside, but she couldn't see anything that should scare her. This was ridiculous. She should put an end to this immediately. She pulled the closet door open quickly, stepping in. She heard a snap. Something fell on her. She closed her eyes and raised her hands above her head. It felt hard and yet something cool was running down her head, her dress, continually moving. She backed away and threw her head forward, her hands slapping and brushing at whatever was on her. And when she opened her eyes, she saw dirt. Dirt on her hands, dirt on the floor, all over her dress, her shoulders. Cold dirt. And on the floor in front of her, a broken doll. A quarter of its porcelain head was missing, eliminating one eye, and the other eye was completely black. Scratches all over its face, marring its fake peach complexion. A perfect—picture perfect—dress of bright colors was on it. Dead leaves, grass, dirt everywhere. And the doll lying on the floor with no eyes to stare up at her. But it did stare.

Emma realized she wasn't breathing. She clutched at her heart, then her throat. She couldn't feel anything but cold. Her legs backed her away awkwardly, jerkily, the rest of the way out of the closet until she hit her bed.

She couldn't tear her eyes away from the doll. It had no mouth. Just a gaping hole, broken, cracks traveling up one cheek, down the chin. Even in its hideous state, for some inconceivable reason, it looked like it was going to move on its own. She could swear it. At any moment it would get up and attack her. Her vision was blurring and darkening. She couldn't move to get out of her room and into the hall, couldn't scream for help. She fell to the floor. Now she was at its level.

Was that a movement? Did it move?

Emma couldn't even crawl away. Her nails dug into the floorboards.

Her vision went black and she heard racing footfalls.

Her head said, *The doll the doll the doll...*

*

Faint voices.

Downstairs.

Emma was groggy, very groggy, and had no desire to open her eyes. Her brain felt as if it was a clean white surface with no cares or responsibilities.

Then she remembered.

The doll appeared in her head and looked so lifelike, she screamed. She thought she screamed. She felt so disconnected, she wasn't sure she really had.

Footfalls pounding the steps.

Christopher bounded in, throwing the door open.

"Emma, what happened?" he asked, grabbing her hands and sitting down hard next to her on the bed.

Bed... Wasn't I on the floor? How did I get to the bed?

Emma felt her mouth moving but heard nothing come out of it. When Christopher ran one hand along her forehead, she felt wetness. She must have been sweating.

"Emma, the doctor's given you an injection to keep you calm. He was worried you might be upset when you woke up." Christopher paused. He seemed unsure. Abigail stood behind him, looking at her with an intensity she couldn't discern as anything more than fervent. "Emma," Christopher continued carefully, "I found you on the floor outside Abigail's room. It was very strange. There was a lot of...dirt. And...you were holding a broken doll."

Emma's mind couldn't quite comprehend what Christopher had just said. *Holding?* She'd been *holding* it? That wasn't possible. That would mean... Wouldn't it mean...

Emma felt her eyes roll back in their sockets and her hand lose its grip of Christopher's.

February 20, 1861

The doctor diagnosed Emma with hysteria, which he explained was a relatively common disease among females. He said there was no other explanation for her constant fainting spells. She couldn't stay awake longer than a few minutes before she fainted again. She had to be taken to a special facility—an asylum, to be exact—to help cure the condition or, at the very least, help her live with it.

Abigail made sure, when they took Emma away, that they brought her "favorite doll" with them. Emma couldn't be without it, she said. Emma needed it for comfort, she said. They were to always—*always*—keep it in Emma's arms, she said. Always.

*

Abigail sat with Christopher for long periods of time reading passages from the Bible. Christopher was inconsolable. He thought there must have been something he could have done to help Emma, some sign that she was going crazy that he had missed. He thought he should have spent more time with her, more time at home in general.

Abigail would read a passage or two aloud, then Christopher would say that he couldn't believe Emma was gone. Abigail would read another passage or two aloud, and Christopher would sob just barely louder than a whisper.

It went on like this for an hour.

Finally, while Abigail was in the middle of a sentence, Christopher stood up, came to her side, and knelt by her chair.

"If it runs in the family…" he began.

She held his cheek in her palm. "It isn't in the family. I'm older than Emma and I'm fine. See? I'm still sitting here, aren't I?"

"Thank God," he breathed out and cried into her dress by her knees. "I'm sure Mother had it too, I'm sure she was on the brink and just hadn't tipped over yet." He sniffed. "Ever since Mother and Father, everything has been wrong, it's all been wrong…"

Abigail didn't hear anything else he said after that. She stroked his head with the hand that wasn't holding the Bible. She pulled very lightly at the hairs on the back of his head. Ran her nails lightly down his hair. Ran one nail harder down the bones at the back of his neck. He didn't notice. He was too busy mourning his sister.

March 12, 1862

Abigail checked the date on her calendar. It had been over a year since Emma's diagnosis—the anniversary date of her admission to the asylum was circled—and the doctors still thought it was best to keep her in the asylum, last she knew. She had shown more and more lucidity, but her paranoia was still extreme. She jumped at shadows, the doctors said, and had to be approached carefully; she trusted no one.

Abigail had visited her now and then, but Christopher visited far more frequently. He would always report on her progress, and Abigail found her mind drifting during those times. In fact, Abigail repeatedly found her mind drifting when she read her Bible, the new one she had bought after the house was just hers and Christopher's. Christopher's and hers. He was so much like Father now. He was so good, so kind, the way Father was before he left. At the top of the stairs, he was so kind, right before...

Abigail heard the front door close and Christopher walked in, seeming agitated.

"What's wrong, Christopher?" she asked. Her cheek twitched. It often did that now.

"They won't let me see Emma," he practically yelled, nervously pacing back and forth across the sitting room floor. He must have stormed past Ashdon—his hat was still in his hands. He hit it against his palm over and over.

"What do you mean?" Abigail asked.

"You know what I mean. This is the third time they've told me I can't see her anymore. That's what I mean," he said harshly. He stopped and put his free hand to his head. "I'm sorry. I'm not angry with you." This is what Father would have been, had he stayed after Mother's death, Abigail was sure. He would have been reasonable, kind.

"Did they give you a reason yet?" Abigail asked.

"All I know is she's taken a bad turn," he said. "Abigail, she was doing so much better. Of course the paranoia was still there, but she hasn't seen any dolls, they've kept them away from her and they've done so much to convince her they aren't alive, they can't hurt her. Nobody will tell me what happened." He sank into his favorite chair.

"We still have her," Abigail said. She didn't see a problem.

"You mean you think she'll be fine?" Christopher asked.

"She's right upstairs," Abigail said.

Christopher frowned. "I just came from the asylum, Abigail, she's not here, she's there."

Abigail shook her head like a schoolgirl. "She's here." Twitch.

Christopher squinted at her. "I don't know what you mean," he said.

Abigail smiled. "I was waiting for the right time to tell you. She looks so pretty, you wouldn't believe it." She noticed Christopher wipe his hand on his trousers. "Don't be upset, you can see her too, if you want."

Christopher swallowed. "I...I would like that, Abigail. Can you...can you show her to me?"

Abigail stood up and took his hand. It was shaking. "You're excited," she said. "I was too, when I first saw her." She led Christopher up the stairs slowly. She walked up each one as if she had to concentrate very hard. She was secretly afraid of falling down them, that Mother would push her down. But she didn't like to say so. She didn't like to make Christopher worry. But this—this would make him happy. She knew it. He missed Emma so.

She reached her room and pushed open the door. "See her?" she asked. She noticed he was looking around the room. Was this his first time in her room? She couldn't remember anymore. She couldn't remember a lot of things anymore, but she felt better for it.

"Abigail," Christopher said, "there's no one here."

Abigail smiled again. Twitch. "Come here." She led him to her bed and picked up a doll, holding it up in front of her.

"See?" Abigail said. "Isn't she beautiful? She looks so good now."

The doll had vibrant blue eyes, pink cheeks, a beautiful dress, and...

Christopher took the doll from Abigail's hands. "This isn't mohair, Abigail," he said, petting the doll's hair. "It... it's..."

"Emma's hair," Abigail said, still smiling. "I visited her a while ago with this doll—it looks just like her, doesn't it? And I put it on her lap while I cut her hair off. She didn't like it—in fact, she screamed and screamed, such a fuss, so I had to leave when I'd only gotten a couple of chunks. Oh, but don't worry. I didn't cut it from where anyone would notice. But look, Christopher, look what I did! I brought her home for you. Look." She pushed the doll into Christopher's chest. "Look." She bit her lip and waited.

Christopher held the doll out and looked at it. "Abigail..." His voice was shaking. It sounded as if he was going to cry. "Abigail, there's scalp attached."

"Well I had to hurry," Abigail said angrily. "And she

kept moving. How could I cut it right when she was moving so much?"

"You tied her hair on with strings," he said, covering his mouth. He squeezed his eyes shut.

"What are you doing?" Abigail asked, pointing at Christopher's face. "Are you going to cry? Don't. Don't do it. It wakes Mother."

"Abigail, we talked about this." His voice was so shaky. "Mother isn't here."

"She's here," Abigail hissed. "Don't say it, she'll come again. She always knows."

Christopher hushed her. "Don't say things like that. You know it's not true. We've talked about—"

"Stop stop stop stop stop," Abigail said. "Now you're upsetting Emma."

Christopher sniffled.

"Don't cry!" she shouted. "You don't know how I suffer when you wake Mother." She brushed off Christopher's shoulder. She knew another of Mother's tears had fallen on it, but she didn't want him to see. "Now," she said more calmly, "aren't you happy to have Emma back?"

Christopher paused, assessing her. "Yes, I've missed her very much," he said cautiously.

"Yes, I thought so," she said.

"Abigail," Christopher said softly, "do you know what I think we should do?"

"What?" Abigail asked.

"I think we should visit Emma in the asylum," he said carefully.

"You have her in your hands," she said. "And you said downstairs that they won't let anyone see her."

"Yes, but now that we have this beautiful doll, I know

they'll let us see her," Christopher said. "And then she'll be so happy."

Abigail thought for a moment. Her head was always so clouded now, it was hard to figure out what she should do. Mother said not to, so Abigail knew it was a good idea.

"Yes, let's do that," Abigail said. "Then perhaps they'll give me the rest of her."

Part 3

I am weary with my groaning; all the night make I my bed to swim; I water my couch with my tears.

Psalm 6:6
King James Bible

March 13, 1862
Christopher Whitestone's diary

Today I am the last Whitestone left alive or sane. I cannot send a letter to tell Father about the tragedy of his daughters. Nobody knows where he is, if he's living or dead. And so I am alone. And I am so alone.

Emma was the greatest loss to me; she was sweet and kind and loving. But Abigail was a different kind of loss. I thought that somehow I could fix her with gentle treatment, the opposite of Mother's harsh ways, and give her more attention than Father did. I thought perhaps she could change if only she saw that she, too, could be loved by someone within our family. But as her condition worsened quickly over time, my assurances and comforting did less and less to help her.

Emma was always wary of Abigail, and I think Abigail felt that. But I did try to make up for it all. I have failed, and now any softness that Abigail may have had is gone. She is also alone, but she is trapped inside her mind. At least that is what the doctors say. She is being kept in a room next to Emma's. I do not know whether Emma would be pleased with that, but when I visit, it makes me feel as if I am with them in our house again.

When I admitted Abigail, I gave the doctors at the asylum the doll Abigail had thought was Emma. As one of them turned it over in his hands, he realized something was inside. He cut the doll open at its bisque shoulders; dirt and leaves poured out, and something clinked to the floor. It was a key, a key I'd never seen before.

As soon as I got home, I tried the key in every lock until I got to the very last one. I unlocked the door to

Mother and Father's room and opened it for the first time in my life. Dolls both broken and whole, dirt, grass, and dead flowers lined the edges of the bed and dresser. Strewn all over the floor. Everywhere. My head spun with something like an unhinging of the mind and distortion of the eyes in that moment, a disturbance I had never experienced before. I had to sit down on the floor amongst that dreadful mess just to calm myself. Although it was a frightening thing to find, the reason for its heavy effect eluded me. But then I realized: Emma's almost incoherent babbling after her fall —she spoke of a doll and dirt falling on her. I know now— it was Abigail. Abigail had done it on purpose.

So much pain—and all to no end.

I visited the toymaker in town and found out that Abigail had been going there ever since Mother's death and Father's disappearance a year and a half ago, steadily buying dolls. She'd told the clerk to keep it just between the two of them because they were gifts.

They were not gifts. They were for Abigail.

God help me, I never knew my sister, my family.

Do I even know myself?

One after the other the Whitestones have fallen. I fear I will be next and it paralyzes me. I know that I must find Father to prove my paranoia wrong, but I am too afraid to leave. I am so afraid of everything. I am even afraid of this house. I am afraid she is still here. I am afraid because I know. She is.

LETTER TO THE READER

Dearest Reader,

Thank you for delving into the Whitestone family and their dark Victorian world with me. I cannot wait to bring you further into the town and share even more suspenseful stories with you. You are a valued friend, and I hope you'll come along on the journey with me.

If you have suggestions as to what you'd like to see in the Dark Victoriana Collection, tweet me, Facebook me—contact me! I will respond to your messages and listen to your ideas. You are the reason I write.

Thanks again for giving an independent author a chance, and please leave a review on Amazon and Goodreads if you enjoyed *Anatomy of a Darkened Heart*. See you in the next book!

~ Christie Stratos

Connect with me on YouTube, Instagram, Facebook, Twitter, Goodreads, and more!

**CONTINUE THE DARK VICTORIANA
COLLECTION WITH BOOK 2:**

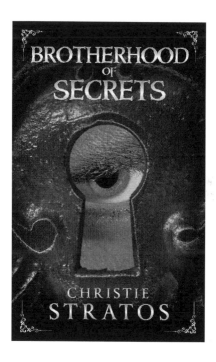

"Brothers in the art of keeping secrets." This is the mantra Mr. Locke's carefully chosen five employees must repeat together every day before starting work.

Day by day, each of these young, single, alone-in-the-world workers is being molded into the family they crave. A family in which each member has his use toward an end he doesn't even know exists.

How do the brotherhood and the town's secrets interlock? Only Mr. Locke holds the key.

**Read as a standalone novel or an expansion of the
Whitestone legacy. Available now.**

MEET THE AUTHOR

Christie Stratos is an award-winning writer who holds a degree in English Literature. She is the author of *Anatomy of a Darkened Heart* and *Brotherhood of Secrets*, the first two books in the Dark Victoriana Collection. Christie has had short stories and poetry published in Ginosko Literary Journal, Andromedae Review, 99Fiction, and various anthologies. An avid reader of all genres and world literature, Christie reads everything from bestsellers to classics to indies.

Printed in Great
Britain
by Amazon